Ghosteria

Volume Two: the Novel
Zircons May Be Mistaken

Ghosteria

Volume Two: the Novel
Zircons May Be Mistaken

Tanith Lee

IMMANION PRESS
Stafford England

Ghosteria Volume Two: The Novel:
Zircons May Be Mistaken
By Tanith Lee
© 2014

Cover by Danielle Lainton & Storm Constantine from an idea by Tanith Lee
Layout by Storm Constantine

Set in Palatino Linotype

ISBN 978-1-907737-63-3

IP0119

New (future) Author Web Site, as the original has been stolen:
http://www.tanith-lee.com

An Immanion Press Edition
http://www.immanion–press.com
info@immanion–press.com

Books by Tanith Lee

A Selection from her 93 titles

The Birthgrave Trilogy (The Birthgrave; Vazkor, son of Vazkor,
Quest for the White Witch)
The Vis Trilogy (The Storm Lord; Anackire; The White Serpent)
The Flat Earth Opus (Night's Master; Death's Master; Delusion's
Master; Delirium's Mistress; Night's Sorceries)
Don't Bite the Sun
Drinking Sapphire Wine
The Paradys Quartet (The Book of the Damned; The Book of the
Beast; The Book of the Dead; The Book of the Mad)
The Venus Quartet (Faces Under Water; Saint Fire; A Bed of Earth;
Venus Preserved)
Sung in Shadow
A Heroine of the World
The Scarabae Blood Opera (Dark Dance; Personal Darkness;
Darkness, I)
The Blood of Roses
When the Lights Go Out
Heart-Beast
Elephantasm
Reigning Cats and Dogs
The Unicorn Trilogy (Black Unicorn; Gold Unicorn; Red Unicorn)
The Claidi Journals (Law of the Wolf Tower; Wolf Star Rise, Queen
of the Wolves, Wolf Wing)
The Piratica Novels (Piratica 1; Piratica 2; Piratica 3)
The Silver Metal Lover
Metallic Love
The Gods Are Thirsty

Collections

Nightshades
Dreams of Dark and Light
Red As Blood – Tales From the Sisters Grimmer
Tamastara, or the Indian Nights
The Gorgon
Tempting the Gods
Hunting the Shadows
Sounds and Furies

Also Published by Immanion Press
The Colouring Book Series

Greyglass
To Indigo
L'Amber
Killing Violets
Ivoria
Cruel Pink
Turquoiselle

Ghosteria Volume 1: The Stories

The grave's a fine and private place,
But none I think do there embrace.

To His Coy Mistress
Andrew Marvell
(1621 - 1678)

PART ONE

1

The Scholar

Elizabeth has said we all live in a yellow submarine. At the time, the young faces of Coral and Laurel looked blank. And the Knight, as ever, just looked bemused, knowing it was nothing he would ever comprehend, although he didn't care so long as Elizabeth kept talking. I'm afraid I too didn't grasp her reference for a minute or so. I'm that foolish combination, both too old a man – and too *young* – always to comprehend. Then I recalled it was a Ringo Starr song, a Beatles song, from way back, that fine band who reintroduced the world of popular music to many wonderful and, to my mind, classical musical modes, chords and references.

But, aside from all else, Elizabeth's statement is completely wrong in so many ways. Since it isn't a submarine, it's a house, though yellowish, I suppose, like a fading autumn leaf. Part of it, obviously, in the distant past, was the old fortress-castle that once stood alone here on the hill. (I hazard too 'fortress-castle' is tautology. Maybe not, in this case.) And we don't exactly live here, either. 'Bivouac' might be a better word. Perch in mid-flight, between catastrophes, yearn and wait. But for what had we waited, we five, all this while? For Now, I think. For exactly Now.

Egomaniacally, I'll explain about myself, first. If you will permit.

I did not, originally, reside here, but in a frankly bloody awful 'flat' in London – one room with kitchenette, and a lavatory in a cupboard – 'shared bath' down the hall. (Shared bath? I never *shared* a bath with anyone, except the tin one with my tiny brother, when I was nearly as tiny, he two and I four. We used to laugh and splash each other and swim ducks made of – was it? – rubber. While our very nice mother laughed too, and we were all happy. Dear little Eddy, my sibling, died when he was ten. Meningitis, rare and often wrongly diagnosed then, but still a possible. Then it was a bath of tears. Our mother died only three years after. Where did they go, these, my darlings? Insane, isn't it. I am *here*. But where are *they*?

However, although well into my ninety-sixth or seventh year, (I can never quite recall now which), I was still pretty hale and healthy, and despite being evicted at seventy from my post as Advisory Librarian at Murchester, (where I had had a much nicer flat of three spacious rooms, with kitchen and bathroom, plus the service of a cleaner called Mr Timp), I kept up *my* services when they were required. Mine was often interesting work, and besides augmented my rather frugal pension.

I arrived at this house in the spring of 2011, and anticipated being here about three to four months, as the library is a large one. It lies, of course, in that smaller part of the house that is still solid, and until recently well-maintained. A curious combination inside of ancient show rooms, kept almost as when they had first been created, in the sixteen or seventeen hundreds, if not, actually, *quite* perfectly replicated. But also there were modern rooms, centrally heated and with delightful clean running water, flush lavs and electric kettles. Oh, those were the days.

By the second week I was well into my work, and enjoying myself enormously, sorting out the rambling library during the morning and the evening, taking time before lunch to walk the – then elegant – gardens, or cautiously to explore the more ruinous other premises. The whole place was said to be haunted. I must say I'd never, at that time I was originally ninety-six or seven, ever seen a ghost. Nor did I, during those two weeks. But there were plenty of tales about them, even in some of the reference works I had been cataloguing. A man in a green coat upstairs, while a warrior in chain mail, he from around the 1300's, was said to roam the ruins, maintaining sentry-go; he had even been spotted now and then over in the more – to him – futuristic areas, staring about him, it was said, in apparent puzzled fascination, at the real 17th century armchairs and the faux 18th century statues. A very young girl – or two of them – in perhaps Victorian dress were also said to appear from time to time in a corridor, or on the big stair that led from the hall. But I never saw her, either one, Neither any, in fact. Not then.

Week three dawned bright and sunny with a splash of golden late summer weather. I'd planned to start on some of the very oldest books that day, tomes of colossal size and inclined to damp, for which, probably, they would have to be professionally treated elsewhere. The weather though delayed me. I went for my walk rather early, and rather long, and admired rabbits bounding through the slightly overgrown kitchen garden, their nice round mouths full of pilfered lettuce. The damsons were coming on well, I remember, and I ate a crimson windfall apple. Yes, my old strong teeth had stayed good enough for that. They used to say that how your teeth are, your bones go too. Although I've known plenty who lost their teeth and had bones of steel. Perhaps it was the reverse, in my case, but I'd had no trouble till then, aside from the odd slight twinge of winter rheumatism.

I drank a glass of wine with my lunch. But then, in this house, I often did. Then I returned, about two-thirty, to the library, and started in again on those grand damp old books.

It was the grandest, biggest and dampest, I'm afraid. A great monster of a volume, about one foot by one and a half, and a good four inches thick, covered in stained tobacco-brown leather with light mould in verdigris patches. I could just reach it without needing the library step – even in my nineties I was still just on six feet. I tried to be gentle, but it wouldn't come, you see. The book seemed to want to stay exactly where it was, and rot in its own good time. *You leave me alone, you old fool,* it might have said. *I'm almost two centuries older than you. Defer to your elders and betters.* Somehow feeling this from it, I accordingly stepped back, and then maybe it changed its mind. Or I'd just dislodged it enough, I suppose. Right then it seemed like enemy action.

Off the shelf it charged, straight at me, and into my upturned face. It crashed against my nose, and then there was an instant of nothing, only there seemed to have been a huge sound, rather than a blow, and next came the second blow as – thrown backward – my skull hit the thinly-carpeted stone paving of the library floor.

I came to, as I thought, in the early evening. The windows were glowing twilight blue.

At first I was dazed, then frightened. Any staff that were at the house knocked off about three o'clock, leaving me to my own devices. And here I had lain, unnoted, and presumably concussed, and with a broken nose – Yet, to my complete surprise, I was in no pain, could see perfectly well, was not even dizzy. To my anxious hands my face felt exactly as ever, and when, cautiously, I sat up, and then got to my feet, I seemed to have suffered no injury, let alone any trauma. I walked carefully across the floor, flexing my arms and legs, moving my head, breathing, I thought, deeply – and all was well. I was fine. Entirely still myself.

It was only when I turned round to see what had happened to the huge old book that had attacked me, that I saw instead my own dead body lying, broken, on the Turkish rug.

Situation Report

The Terror began at the very end of 2019 – New Year's Eve. By February of 2020, it was established and, seemingly 'non-negotiable'. Who, after all, can reason with a corpse? Even a pseudo-living one. But by then I had, evidently, been for nearly nine years, a ghost – not remotely therefore in any way like a corpse. I seemed, to myself, or those portions of myself I was by now to see, (a view in a mirror no longer being possible), as I had become in my nineties. I was also the same height, ostensibly the same apparent weight, and of the usual gaunt if big-boned frame.

The others too, visually, are like the selves they were in the days immediately before their deaths. But I'll come to that.

Meanwhile, what we could see of the Terror, and the –

things – they that the Terror had coined, they were just as corpselike as all our own corpses must become, after being carted off, (as mine was on the morning following my demise, once one of the poor house-staff had stumbled over my remains in the library), to a handy grave.

There is a name for the creatures of the Terror, of course. They had been current for hundreds of years in various forms, but were thought to be a supernatural legend, an *idea* rather than a likelihood. Admittedly, quite early on in the 21st century, as I recollect – rather an amount of Science Fantasy literature, and even films (or 'movies') had been produced, based on the premise.

However, it was quite another matter when one saw for oneself, and was reliably told it was real. Even the calm and frequently pragmatic Elizabeth let out a cry when first we glimpsed the advent on one of the house TVs. The TV, (like most of its kind), had a multitude of channels. In the old days these mostly conveyed a lot of pure rubbish, or – even when worthy in themselves – programmes drained of all sense or power by endless over-explanation, over-celebrity appearance, and attention-deficit editing – which meant any decent scene was over in fifteen seconds or less while, where commercially run, approximately thirty minutes of advertising had to accompany twenty-five of actual content. I had seldom bothered with any TV for years, unless I could access an old film – the original version of *The Postman Always Rings Twice*, or *Tinker, Tailor, Soldier, Spy* from the earlier 2000's. These, I hasten to add, on non-comm-channels. Post death, I thought I would not even be able to activate a button. For I had quickly found that, though I could touch my own body, this same body would pass through most objects of substance, from a table to a tree. But it seemed one could perform a type of telekinetic trick with electronics, which Elizabeth demonstrated how to perform, (she too did not trouble with the computers; she had missed their advent). For this reason of (presumed) telekinetics, we were able to turn lights on and off, and radios and TVs too. (Fairly predictably, we seldom attempted much else. Unable, nor needing, to eat or drink, get warm or cool down, bathe, or wash our garments, the relevant adjacent devices were of no use to any of us).

To return to the fundamental point, nevertheless, (I have read, and studied, demonstrably too often among the more leisurely texts), we saw *them*. The Terror. The Plague. The Zombies. And that was exactly what they were, and are.

Mankind has always died from stupid accidents, (myself, for example), or war, (the poor knight), or the wickedness of others, (Coral), or else by biological means – the *normal* plagues, (such as the influenza epidemic of 1918 that carried off the physical being of Laurel), or by our own despairing and disillusioned hands, (Elizabeth). After that, most of us seem to go on our own way into some other 'life', or to, one hopes, kind and serene oblivion. A few, for whatever confused or dedicated reasons, remain where we fell – or where most, or most significantly, we were happy. But the jettisoned bodies decay. They are – *were* – buried, or otherwise destroyed. The sensible dustbins of law, animal need, and time, dispose of them.

Not so with the Terror. These things, patently devoid of anything that might be termed soul, let alone *mind*, roam the landscape, here and – by now, it seems –

everywhere about the world.

What they are, God (or if not God, maybe Nothing) knows. But an impulse they are, a brainless and despirited one, intransigently housed in a yet-operational machine of flesh and bone. Able to wreak havoc and death in turn. Able, in turn, to infect and annexe, swelling their army of the damned. Which then is ever intent to obliterate and amalgamate, probably, *everything*.

They are the ultimate insult of some Satanic or Jehovan Curse upon the race of Men.

Not merely to kill us all, but to remake us as the clay without the substance, the force without either conscience or true Will.

Ghosts are not like these evil and disgusting unmanned tanks of Hell.

Ghosts are only – heart and mind and, perhaps partially, soul; smoke and sighing, music and silence, memory, sorrow, and love.

But the Terror is Hate. Lacking even passion to excuse it.

2

Elizabeth

I killed myself because I could.

Pretty simple, yes?

I was happiest in my early thirties. A lot is talked about the 1960's and Free Love, and the accessibility of the Pill, but it certainly wasn't just that. I'd had a happy childhood, my mother a musician (piano), my father a businessman who loved concerts and theatre. They were great, these parents, attractive and clever and kind, which I gather is an unusual combination. Lucky little Lizzie.

I did the pre-ordained stuff, but not university. I didn't want to. I played (piano too) with a small classical orchestra up near Wales, and painted. That was my real need. Painting, and later, to a limited but for me fulfilling extent, sculpture. I earned enough for a little town flat. But I had an income from my parents. (I said, didn't I, luck unusually good.) My father's benefice came via his Will.

My dad died at forty-one. Heart. (The love of music had made it swell too much maybe – even back then, forty-one was premature.) My mother grieved but survived. Remarried. *She* lived into her eighties. In fact, (ha!) she outlived me by a couple of decades.

I was born about 1933. (Funny thing is, I can never now quite remember if it *was* '33, or '32 – or even, '34 – but near enough.) So I was a kid, a 'little girl', when the Second World War opened its jaws on us all. And now, another odd thing. Because as a kid I wasn't too freaked out. My parents managed to keep calm, you see, and that kept *me* calm. And anyhow, we moved out of London fairly soon. By the time I was seven and a half, (thereabouts), we were northwest, living in a little village full of dolls' houses and sheep, and pretty as a flower, whose name, in English, meant *Cherries*.

The first time I ever saw *this* place, I mean here, where now I am, was with my parents. We visited it, a site of Historic Interest. The war had ended a while before that, and we were moving again, but not right back down south, just southward somewhat, to make London a bit easier of access for my mother occasionally, and Dad a lot. I wondered afterwards if all that travelling, all those gaps of not being with us, helped make my father die. I was almost sixteen when it happened. I remember I'd bought him a present, (crazily his birthday fell only a few days after mine.) I kept it for years, the present, still wrapped up. It was a faithful copy of the original score of a Mozart aria, belonging to the *Queen of the Night*. Or... I think it was the QotN... Being dead can make you forgetful, and sometimes of those most special things you dearly want to recall. I don't know why. I've heard the others say so. It isn't just me.

So then. This fairly-well-orientated child who, presumably, despite a sad premature bereavement, and the re-wedding of her mother, grew up into a confident adult. How did this kid finish by killing herself at exactly the same age her father had been when Death broke him in two over one cruel skeletal knee?

Well I was happy in my twenties, too, and in my early thirties I sort of took wing. I was young enough, and attractive, and I had lovers when I wanted them. And my work, the painting and sculpture, were getting some recognition, and also earning quite well. I was never snobby. I was happy to do book-jackets too, album covers and posters, and a few portraits. I had several quite successful exhibitions in Cardiff and Manchester, and eventually two in London. My statue of Daphne turning into a shrub, (to escape from the lustful god Apollo), was put up in Greenwich Park, near the Meridian. Although unfortunately, there was a fault with something in the plinth and in the hurricane of 1987 Daphne, part verdure or not, was blown right off and smashed in chunks. Of course, I'd been smashed off my plinth a few years myself, by then. I saw it on TV here, about the statue, and thought I didn't care. But later – can ghosts cry? This one can. It just seemed so *mean*, somehow. Mean of something. A stupid way to think.

Anyway, I was thirty-seven when I met Steven. He was thirty-six, tall and strong, with a lion's mane of thick, pale brown hair down to his shapely bum. I used to love that, you know. Not bums, necessarily. The way the men had been enabled to grow their hair long, and wear lace shirts and stuff like that. It seemed an age of grace but it didn't last. Not much does.

Steven and I got together at once. As I said I'd had plenty of lovers by then, no strings, a terrific time had by all, and very few harsh partings. But with Steven it was different. He moved in with me at my little pad at Blackheath.

One wonderful summer. I won't describe it. If you've ever had a summer like that, you'll know. And if you haven't, well that's a shame, and I'm not going to upset you. Don't be jealous. After summer the gold leaves fell and the nights drew in like vultures, and my latest exhibition was cancelled due to 'Lack of Interest'. And Steven, who had charmingly and appreciatively and extravagantly lived off me, turned sullen and unpleasant and next met somebody else. He and the autumn left Blackheath together. I think he and his new lover went to live in Paris. I hope the fucking Eiffel Tower fell on the pair of them. (Though it probably didn't. Even dead, I'd maybe have heard.)

Oh, you say, so you went into a Gothic decline over lost love and pined away for three or four years and then ended it all. It wasn't that straightforward. It wasn't just love and summer that ended. The exhibition was the first, and then the book illustration contract, that was also cancelled, and the burglar broke in and wrecked the place, and the mess-up with my allowance 'happened', so I ceased to get it, and my mother was shrieking down the phone from her house in Spain that I was a parasite and she couldn't afford to keep me any more. And the money Steven had stolen out of my account, that too, around seven thousand pounds. And the leak in the kitchen roof I couldn't afford to fix. And breaking two of my fingers, (index, middle), on my right hand when a piece of metal resisted the electric tool I was using and erupted, crushing them, and they didn't mend straight, and it wasn't the awful way they looked, I didn't care too much about that – just that I couldn't work properly any more. Not that, by then, anybody seemed to want my work.

My fortieth birthday arrived, and it was just as if those three bridging years had all been one. One long winter of short hopeless days and frozen nights. My 'friends' had all gone too, flown off like migrating birds who avoid the initial contaminating touch of frost. No friends. No lovers. No family. There were four or five bad paintings I did, that looked as if a demented and talentless child had made them. I'd left my flat by then. Had to. Just a room. That sort of thing. Over a main road that roared and screamed and provided violent accidents – as my neighbours said, from four a.m. until four the next morning.

On my birthday I took myself, all alone – I couldn't budget for anyone else, nor was there anyone, to a beautiful restaurant I'd sometimes formerly gone to in Putney. The meal was delicious, wine fine. Everyone was happy. Everyone else. Those strangers at other tables. But I did my best, and then went home quite early, on the racketing train smelling of other people's inebriation, excited hope, and utter exhaustion.

I got another job that year. I worked in a big store that sold everything and nothing, in the novelties department. No, I'm not even going to talk about it.

You do what you can, if you can, when and how you can. Somewhere, as forty ticked away towards forty-one, a man picked me up in a cafe, and when I realised I really was expected to sleep with him, couldn't, and wouldn't, I escaped in a cab. The driver was mad and kept on telling me the world was going to end soon, and I said, "Good". But that meant nothing to him, and his prophecy nothing to me. (It was almost fifty years ahead of its time any way.)

I didn't celebrate my forty-first birthday.

But I dreamed about my father as by then I hadn't for years. He looked old and frail and unhappy. He said I had betrayed him, I was a bitch, a monster. I had caused his heart attack by my unspeakable (and unspecified) crimes and nastinesses.

This dream was so unjust, so hideous, I couldn't shake it. I was forty-one, and he had *been* forty-one. Had anything about his death *been* my fault? What? How? *When*? Perhaps he had mistaken me for my mother, who had changed so much she had become unknown to me, and with whom, since the 'parasite' business, I had had no contact. But I wasn't like her. I was like Dad. My dad. My dad.

I don't know how long it went on. I've heard about it since, that sort of weakening and inertia. Decline and fall. I killed myself with sleeping tablets and gin in the spring of 1970-something. Can't remember quite the year – '73? '4? '5? But I was forty-one. Was I? Yes, I was forty-one.

It didn't hurt. I wasn't afraid. I thought I'd sleep forever. But I woke up *here*.

And why *here*, this place part castle, part old mansion, part past and part present? Like a glowing sunny yellow submarine floating in a murky subterranean sea, far down below the margins of life and the world.

It was when I was about fifteen, (thirteen?), around then. My mother had read about the house and semi-attached ruined fort in some book, and said we might go and see it. My father liked old houses too, and so we went. That is, we came here, and saw.

I can remember it in the sunshine, a spring afternoon. There had been rain, but that stopped. Now rain drops only sparkled in the trees and on the grass and shrubs as we approached, uphill, and the sun was fully out. Frankly, easy-going and pleased teenager that I was, I liked travelling anywhere. Especially with them, my pretty, elegant mother and handsome father who, though 'something in the city', looked more like an actor from the

Old Vic, or (a later era still to come) Olivier's theatre on the South Bank.

I don't remember all of it, the house. I know I liked it back then.

It seemed, we were told, from the 1600's until Victorian times, the house had been owned by a single continuing family. Holland, I think, was their name.

We went round the big rooms with their recreated semi-souls, the occasional anachronisms, or other things not quite right – none of which, then, I took in or criticised; my father I suspect did see and note them, but did not spoil the adventure by pontificating. My mother probably did not notice anything amiss. Her yardstick would be Hollywood movie-sets. Brilliant pianist, but a bit of a soppy date, my mother, frankly. (And I only began to see *that* plainly in my twenties, though other things rather earlier.) There were too however, extraordinary moments at the house, of the ancient, even the eldritch. A portrait-hung corridor, for example, (posed Holland on Holland), that began around 16-something, and then wound down into the castle end, changing, galvanised, into pure blank stone, and a round room at the end, with arrow-slits filled by aquamarine shards of sky. Below, the tumble of the far side of the hill. And woods beyond. From here they had fired out the bladed shafts to kill and maim any enemy approaching. The room impressed me. Some memory seemed caught in it. Anger and determination... God knew. But there had been feuds and to spare in the castle's past.

Later, when we'd done the indoor tour, we thought, before 'doing' the gardens, we'd have one of the cream teas in the tearooms – not to be missed – there was still post-war rationing, and real local cream and jam would be a treat indeed.

My father went ahead and my mother and I stopped at a discreet 'Ladies' to one side, just off the main house hall. (Later, before I – *came back*, as it were – these buildings, loos and orangery and café, were closed and turned into offices for the admin and recreation of the restored house.)

I wanted to comb my hair, which I'd started to wear rather long. My mother, bored and thirsty, left me to it. When I came out, I paused a moment in the hall, and glanced up the great sturdy flex of the stairway. Oddly, or maybe not, no one else was there right then. And then, someone was.

She was standing about halfway up the stair, and I noticed that where she stood, somehow, was a dark crimson runner or carpet, with ornate goldeny edges, which had not, and still was not, apparent anywhere else on the stair. But this sort of melted out, and then there was only the girl, standing, looking at me in a quietly bemused way.

I thought she was about my age – thirteen, fifteen, something like that. But she was dressed in the sort of clothes I now know belonged some thirty years before. A deep blue costume, long straight skirt just clear of her ankles, a little, waisted jacket and a white blouse. Her rich brown hair, unlike mine, was firmly pinned up on her head. Her grey eyes were sober, and sad.

"Hello," I said. But I was rather uneasy. I thought there might be a party going on, fancy-dress, and therefore I was certainly out of bounds, and intruding. She didn't answer. She shook her head, very gently, as if to say, I'm sorry, but I don't speak your language. And she turned, and went up the stair – or she began to. After

I think three steps, she vanished. It wasn't like the carpet, that soft melt-away. One second she was visible, quite real, human. And then... nobody was there.

I was a bit quiet over our tea. And when we went out to see the gardens, I wasn't concentrating entirely, though I remember the fruit trees, all pruned (hacked) back, as if they should never be allowed to properly produce blossom, or leaves, let alone fruit, again. (Of course, they would. Some of them are still here, wild now, and very active.)

Next it began to rain again. We beat it to the car, and drove off, only stopping once at a pub, (adults were allowed to drink and drive then), for a couple of gins for my parents and some lemonade concoction for me.

It was in the evening, two or three hours after we had got home. The night was turning chill, but the woman who 'helped out' had laid a fire in the sitting room. My father had lit it, and my mother had drunk a sherry on top of the two gins, and gone prettily to sleep on the sofa.

My father said to me, "Are you all right, Lizzie? You've been a bit quiet, haven't you?"

I sat, and looked at him, and then I said, "I think I saw a ghost."

Unlike Mum, who would have, in friendly amusement, mocked me and laughed, he only widened his beautiful dark eyes and said, "Really? You lucky girl. I suppose this was in the house?"

"Yes." I told him, without adornment, or shyness, about the girl in the long blue skirt, the melting runner, the vanishment.

He listened, watching me closely and attentively in a way he had, not – never – as if trying to fault or catch me out, but as if not to miss a single nuance of my emotion and reaction.

When I'd finished, he sighed, He looked down at his hands, lying quietly together. "As I said, lucky. What a wonderful thing to have seen – to have been *able* to see. Not everybody *can* see ghosts, you know. I never have. I'm jealous – no, I'm not. I admire you. Well done, Lizbeth. You make me proud."

A couple of days I think after, I asked him what he thought a *ghost* really was. He said it might be a variety of things. Some were recordings on the air, a sort of photograph taken and sometimes stored, due to enormous passion, or horror, or even love, on the lens of time, and kept for a long while, or even forever perhaps, in that area where the powerful moment had occurred. But other types of ghosts truly did seem to be the personalities – if not the actual spirits – of people who had died there, or even elsewhere, he had heard of this too – but they came back to that spot – that particular hill or street or house, because it had for them some special meaning. And then again it seemed some ghosts really were the life force, the soul or spirit, that had lingered. Either it didn't credit its physical life was done, and so went on acting it out until, eventually one hoped, it got the message and moved on. Or else it had simply been so happy there it insisted on remaining a few years, or centuries, longer. And if it had been traumatised, the same thing might happen too. It was unable to escape – which was where some form of exorcism might be helpful.

How gracious and how magical he was, that man. My father. How I loved him. I don't think I ever, while I lived, loved anyone, even Steven – when I *did* love him –

so well, so deeply. But he died, my dad. And if he haunted anywhere, I never found it. Perhaps, even though he'd loved me, he was just glad to get completely free of it all, and us, me too, in the end.

Yet obviously that's why I came back here after I died: my father and the visit to the house. What he said. His sweetness .

I hadn't meant to do anything like this. *Nothing* was further from my plans. Or – *nearer*. I *wanted* Nothingness. A bit of peace.

But there was a kind of gliding, as if, half asleep, my bed, or the train carriage I was seemingly snoozing in, was skating calmly through the depths of night. And in a while I 'woke up', there is no other way I can describe it. And here I was.

I wandered a while through the house and into the ruins and around the gardens and the hill. And when the sun rose I went indoors and sat on a chair, which naturally I didn't at all do, since we pass *through* furniture and everything else; it takes an act of will, even unconsciously, to keep us even standing or walking on the floors or the ground. Not difficult, only peculiar...

I wasn't frightened. I knew what had happened. And in a while more I met the others, or at least the two girls; Laurel, who I'd seen before in my teens when she had stood on the staircase, then turned, gone up three stairs and vanished. And Coral, who had died some time before Laurel, as Laurel had died some fifty-plus years before me. I met the Knight last of all, though he was the first here. And we all met our Scholarly librarian almost forty years after, when the book killed him in the library.

And then, of course, the other thing started.

2020. Year of the Apocalypse.

Progress Report

You'll doubt this, but when I first saw *them* I laughed. Oh, not absolutely at first. That was on the TV news bulletin before the signal failed, and then all electric power went. But when they began to turn up here...

Well, I had nothing to fear, presumably, unlike any live human in a living flesh-and-blood body, who has every physical reason to fear them utterly.

And they *do* look so incongruous.

Clumsy and wilful and repulsive and *useless*.

Staggering along in the woods or through the amok fields, or about on the road. They keep falling over, or crashing into things. Now and then bits of them fall off. They aren't all rotting exactly, though some have gone farther than others before the zomboid force, or whatever one calls it, got them going again

But they have no coordination, no mental power – how could they have? These are the dead without any soul or spirit at all.

Mostly, then, they came and went, floundering about, sometimes even getting into the rampant orchard and flailing through the boughs, fruit raining – and ignored. They rarely caught any animals – or if they did, nine times out of ten they let them go out of sheer discoordination. There was sometimes a single casualty. I try not to think about that. It goes without saying where they got hold of people they tore them up, biting off bits, and left them dead. (Glad to say I only saw examples of that on TV.) But the killed corpses, empty but contaminated with this ridiculous and illogically motivating plague, would presently get up too and start crashing and sprawling about like the originals that had killed them.

They seem to have no real goal. Well, they wouldn't have, would they? No heart, no soul, no brain – just random left-over mental impulses. Of all the deaths that have been visited on the human race, this has to be the most pointless. Grossly disgusting yet utterly inane.

No ghosts seem to have resulted either. No one like the five of us.

Maybe a good thing, that.

There are now a few of *them* anyway, that seem to hang around – whereas mostly, before, they came and went, moving in and then on, in random, lumbering surges.

There are three I've seen a lot of in the past two months. Indescribably repellent, but with odd characteristics. I've given them names. Yes, I'm perverse. I always was, alive or dead.

There's Ugg – he looks to me somehow like a caveman in some old (bad) film. Or Dug – he's always digging at tree roots with what's left of his hands. And Jug, who has jug ears – or only one, now. He appears to have lost the other since I christened him.

So far, they – none of them – have actually properly entered the house. I don't know why not. I suppose it's only a matter of time?

Something to look forward to. (Ha.)

Ha.

3

Laurel

It is rather silly, perhaps, for me to write about myself, even as I was, before I stopped being a physical person. I don't like the word died. I never did, nor any of the odd ways other people employ, as perhaps they still do, to veil over the fact of death. For example, I hate the expression 'passed away', and, much worse, the terms 'gone to God', or 'taken by the angels', as though they had been kidnapped. In a strange fashion it's as if I partly knew that would never happen for me. I was nothing, when living, only an ignorant and unnecessary extra female in our household, where my mother had already borne a daughter and a son for my father. I was a nuisance, then, requiring extra education and extra clothing, and sometimes doctor's visits, and food. I was an expense which, although quite well off, my parents could certainly have done without. While, in other ways, even as I grew, plainly I was never going to be an asset. I was neither clever nor pretty, as, on both counts, my elder sister, Constance, was. I had no talent for singing or the piano, could not efficiently embroider or sew as both my mother and sister could. At my ordinary lessons I was slow. I could not even read passably well until my tenth birthday, and never well aloud. In company I was tongue-tied, as I think they say. I'd blush and stammer, and sometimes, anticipating some party, at Christmas, say, held here in the old house, I would be sick with nervous agitation beforehand. Once I fainted quite away, and in falling broke a flower vase, a favourite of my mother's, quite irreplaceable.

Worse, I bored all my family, particularly my mother and sister since, during my early years, they had to spend more time with me than either my father, or my brother Eric.

Once I heard a woman friend of my mother's acquaintance speak quietly to her when I had just left the room. Hearing my name, maybe instinctively, I hesitated outside the door to listen. It taught me never to eavesdrop, for someone such as myself will rarely hear anything good. "Poor Laurel," said the woman friend. "To come of such a handsome family and to inherit so little from it in either looks or spirit. It must be a great burden, my dear. Still, there is Constance, she'll do well. Where Eric, of course, is a splendid young man."

What my mother said I have no idea, but she will have agreed no doubt, in words, or with one of her heartfelt sighs.

There then, in that silly and pointless manner, I became and was, and grew up to be eighteen years old.

The terrible War had begun, in fact, four years previously, in 1914. Somebody was shot. I could never quite grasp who, or where, because nobody explained it to me. But suddenly there came to be a ferment. Patriotic outcry commenced, and very soon after the urge for all young men to enlist, to give themselves over to Duty. Our enemy was Germany, which circumstance, or so I gather, occurred again in the late 1930's. I hope I have that correctly; I'm afraid I always make mistakes, yet I trust this may be more pardonable following my ousting to a non-physical existence. (I'm not sure non-physical is a proper expression. I've picked up, as they say, rather as one might pick up bits of money, or fruit, from a confusing street, more recent expressions and phrases, by which I mean talk of the later eras that succeeded my very short span. A lot of these came from that thing called a Tea V. No doubt, it's really just my stupidity.)

Eric gave himself up to Duty. Not immediately, but in a while. My mother became used to sitting weeping. She was maddened by the fear that he would die, or be mutilated by shot or shell. This latter option may have seemed worse to her.

As for Constance, she altered into some sort of nurse. I think this was about 1915. She looked quite beautiful in the horrid uniform, naturally. And when at home for her spells of 'leave', she would talk on and on of the dying soldiers whose hands she had held, whispering to them that there was nothing to be afraid of, and how they blessed her for it.

In 1916, despite the Storm and Stress of the War Situation, I had been 'brought out'. I wore a white dress, and had almost fainted again, from fright, before we drove to the event. It was a vast hunt ball, rather muted by the fact that so many of the young were now elsewhere, the males fighting, killing and dying, the females nursing and, too, now and then dying, when the zeppelins had passed over England, like a flock of angry angels Or else, inevitably, overseas in dangerously located hospitals .

Unarguably, I should know so much more about the course and dramatic highlights, a term I think more often, post my era, applied to colouring the hair, of the Great War. But as I've said, I was ignorant, silly, slow, and nobody explained much to me. The brief written images I snatched from the journals left me only more befuddled, and nauseous. (If they had had Tea V then, my stars, it scarcely bears thinking of.) The rationing, even, scarcely touched my family. There were always 'ways and means'.

Eric won some medal. I can't remember what it was for. Conspicuous gallantry, I'm sure. And Constance became engaged to a quite beautiful senior officer, a brigadier or something similar, that she had nursed back to full health from the removal of a chip of bomb-burst lodged in his side. He came of a wealthy and glamorous family, whose heraldic name eludes me, as does his Christian name. I think secretly I called him 'Cuckoo', so debatably his surname might have been Cook-something-or-other.

I feel I must stop this silly chattering. I must – what did they say in the 1920's – no, the 2010's? – *cut to the chaise.*

It was 1918. The War was coming in to land, in a belly-flop, to be quite coarse, and so many stranded in its wake, all broken, poor souls, or lost, and one saw these women, mothers, widows, sisters, weeping in the winter mornings, standing out beyond the house, where the village was back then, with the telegrams in their hands. "Dead," they said, the telegrams. "We regret."

They shivered, the women, and sometimes the men did too, the fathers, sons and brothers or, dare I say this now, the unspoken lovers of those other lost men, ploughed deep into the wine-red blood and midnight mud of France, or wherever it was they were mown down. Or else buried in graves, which were all alike, and like the stone-petrified wooden footprints of the Devil passing over Europe, a Devil that did not exalt but wept and shivered, as the mortal others did, left behind on that frozen timeless shore of grief.

He was called Ashton. Being a soldier, he had some sort of rank, but I can't remember what. There were a lot of soldiers at the dance in the town. I'll call him Captain. I've done that since, always since. Captain Ashton.

The dance was to mark Christmas, and recent Victory, and was held at the Eddington Hall, a lofty stone building with a ballroom of sorts. The big room had been garlanded with paper leaves, and lit with candles in addition to the electricity. I wore a pale dress, and I remember it had a yellow sash, and little yellow flowers worked on the bodice. By then there was a dislike of coupling red to white. I had heard someone remark such a combination was now supposed to be avoided, as it might indicate bandages and fresh blood. Probably they were being 'dramatic', as Eric would have termed it. (Nevertheless, the red-white partnership seemed seldom to be seen, certainly in our part of the country, after the upheavals of 1916).

I remember too I felt less nervous before we left for this dance. Perhaps that was due to my having learned that a tiny secret nip of sherry, from the evening decanter in the dining-annexe, seemed to calm my nerves. (The maids sometimes stole quick nips of sherry too, or the port. No one seemed to notice it. As for me, I had reached the revelation after having a teaspoon of brandy, administered to me by an irritated Constance, when I had wrenched my ankle the previous winter).

Also that evening of the dance I noticed, as if for the first, my arms, mostly bare in the evening frock, also slim and firm, and quite shapely, and luminously pale, if warmer in tone than my dress. Then I noted my eyes were large and clear, and of a shiny grey, the lashes quite long and dark. And my hair, washed carefully the day before, and pinned up with little silvery combs, shone in a wonderful, metallic way. Possibly I was not, then, as unprepossessing as I'd always thought, or been assured, by implication, or family remarks, I was. I had a tiny waist, eighteen inches for my eighteen years. (And for the year; come to that). I never asked myself thereafter if the measurement would increase, by one inch, for every subsequent birthday. Nor would I have the time or space to find out.

When I entered the hall of the dance, everything was as usual. Clusters of young men, cold or timid, and, by this date, some flushed and a touch heightened by alcohol, (it seemed I wasn't the only coward at a social gathering. Of course, the men were brave as lions elsewhere, on the Plains of War). Others were obviously bored, however, scanning the available female meat, just as tired or over-heated lions would be, and thinking: *but these gazelles aren't quite up to scratch, old boy.* For there we were, the straggly gaggle of gazelles, we girls, some also nervous, and some not. Constance began dancing almost as soon as she entered. Her Cuckoo brigadier was absent, in a mud-hole somewhere, waiting valiantly to lead his men into ferocious battle. But Constance had the 'Correct' attitude. She was Brave, and lived every day as it came to her. One must not show worry, must not brood or mutiny. One must set the proper example. And why shouldn't she dance, after all, in her turquoise dress with gilded beadwork? She did her duty. She nursed dying warriors back to health, Saint Constance. I shouldn't say that.

I believe I was starting to lose the spoonful of courage I'd gained after about ten minutes. I would, wouldn't I, have been useless in a battle. Others had been selected from the gazelle herd, borne off in strong lionesque, uniformed, masculine arms, and were dancing now like my sister, yielding and swirling like lilies on a lake.

And I, as ever, sat on my chair, and looked about me brightly, as if loving simply to be there, while my heart drained of its wisp of valour. Until, all at once, he stood before me.

He said his name, and I thought he said that he knew my aunt, one of my aunts, as if he must reassure me he was acceptable. I forget which aunt he was claiming to know. I personally knew none of them well. But he held out his hand, politely, coolly asking me if he might dance with me. So I stood up and said, in my silly small voice, "Of course, Captain." After which he led me out on to the floor, just as a waltz began.

How can I describe him? I don't know. All the words I choose – tall, beautiful, unlike any other – seem entirely mindless, as no doubt, since *I* selected them, then and still, they are. His hair was a flaxen almost white, and his eyes that deep blue one sometimes sees in old paintings of a foreign sea, in Italy, say, or up against the shores of Egypt. He had retained a settled tawny brownness of other places, acquired in hot summer and upheld by the burning winds of winter cold.

I'm not, or I was not, a bad dancer, not really. Light on my feet, somebody had said, and I followed obediently the male lead. Acquiescent cowardice then has its virtues, it seems. Even so, this wasn't what I felt when I danced with this stranger called Captain Ashton. I felt so much more than ever, in my tiny little world of days amounting to eighteen years, I had felt before.

When the music stopped, he led me out of the hall into a side room, where there were chilled drinks – I can't recall what I drank, some sort of lemonade punch, I think, not alcoholic, but very cold. He drank a whisky, just one.

Then we danced again. I can't recall what this dance was. More brisk, I think, than the waltz. We had spoken a few words, both when on the dance floor, and at the draped and pink-paper-flowered tables. The conversation, or rather, the things he said to me, flowed and sank away, what they call, and perhaps did even then, small talk. Yet his intense sea-blue eyes met mine, stared deep within me. Did he do this with all his partners? I don't know how much the war had damaged him, or even if it had sent him mad with that sort of dissimilar but entirely related energy, which I have seen since, in extraordinary acted scenes on the house Tea V, moving photographs, flickers from a later time, when everyone seemed to become more honest, or only more unbearably assaulted by the effort of telling decorous lies.

All told, I conclude we had four dances together, Captain Ashton and I. I learned, or I thought I did, he had a sister, also a nurse as was Constance, and that he had loved France in the two years preceding 1914 when he, then a very young man, had travelled there. What now happened there appalled him, but he kept his statements on this fact to the barest bones; perhaps only one – a single bone of sorrow.

Suddenly it was nearly half past ten o'clock. Another man, this one older, and not in uniform, came up and murmured something to the Captain. The captain nodded, and the man went away.

"You'll have to excuse me," the Captain said to me.

"It's been a great pleasure to meet you. Do take care of yourself. We'll get through this somehow. As the poet says, *The morning always comes*. Goodbye." His voice wasn't cold, nor relieved to be called away; nor was it sorry. He smiled and nodded to me. I said, or I hope I did, the proper polite words. There was something in his eyes, or did I imagine it? – nothing to do with regret at leaving me, only a vague, clear shadow, as if, and I'm unsure how to say this, I had stood for a while between him and something darker and less ordinary. It wasn't that he would miss me, only what I had represented. Or only my interruption of other, more awkward, matters, which help anyone else might have provided him.

I thought, with a stumble of my pulse, that maybe he had been called directly off to return into the Theatre of War. But he did not leave quite then. He went across the room to another group of people, these known to my parents, and quite important in the town. He stood a while with them, sometimes laughing, or gravely listening. He next chose two more girls to dance with. Four dances each, or so I seem to have counted. Just the same as with me. He vanished from the hall some thirty-six minutes after.

My mother had gone in to take supper with her own friends, so I had sat down again, on another chair, and watched the other dancers go past, including, of course, for a time, Captain Ashton. It occurred to me somebody had suggested he dance with me and take me for a lemonade, to even the score for me a little.

After he had completely disappeared, I began to feel cold quite soon, and then very heavy. Shivering, I put on my wrap. Nobody else had or did ask me to dance. At twenty minutes past midnight Constance, who had an early shift at the hospital next day, came over and suggested we should leave. The Findlays would bring Mother home, and besides I was looking washed-out. I think that was how she put it, unless again that is another expression I've somehow accumulated since; washed-out, like an old and fraying shirt or petticoat, all my colours and my usefulness soaked and rubbed and wrung away.

During the night at first I couldn't sleep. Then, when I did, I woke over and over, sometimes with great jumps of fear that had no proper source. Once I woke and I was boiling hot and soaked in perspiration.

Then, as I lay and cooled and calmed, my brain seemed to clear in quite a crystalline manner, and deep within my mind I knew that I would soon hear from Captain Ashton, and we would meet again, and be sworn lovers; we would marry in due course. The War next would have ended, nor would there ever be another, and he and I would love each other through a vibrant youth and holy maturity into a serene and gentle old age.

Never, truly I believe, did I ever before feel so uplifted and so sure, nor so perfectly, radiantly happy, in all my miniature life.

I've never forgotten this, of course not. And perhaps not surprisingly. These were the last definite physical thoughts and feelings I ever had.

That terrible epidemic, that plague, that thing called the Spanish Influenza, was already threading and surging through our world. And so it had come, unseen and unnoticed, into mine. That alarming and radiant night I was already dead, even if I breathed still, and so never knew.

There's no point in recounting the stages of the fever

and horror and decline, nor all those symptoms, and other awfulness, not even the sound of my mother screaming in lament, which I heard as if far, far off on the edge of a mountain, and through thick white fog, when they apparently told her I could not be saved. I can't understand what made her so distressed to lose me. She had never found me in the first place. To her I was nothing. Perhaps it was the thought of the waste of time and money to be entailed in my funeral. I won't retract this statement.

Other Things

We had lived here in the old house all my life, and presumably I didn't know enough about anywhere else to go back to. I'd never been to France, or Italy. I'd never even been to London, let alone Heaven. As for Hell, well, in a soft and insipid way, it was here at home, wasn't it? I'm sorry, no doubt I never grasped how historic this house is, and how lucky I was to live here, and now I'm afraid I still don't grasp it, or appreciate it, as I should, or really care, and anyway I don't live here now, do I? I'm dead here.

It was like wandering back in from a mist, or the fog I spoke of, and I found myself standing in my blue tailored suit, on the stair, and I looked down and there was this pretty, dark-haired young girl below in the hall, and everything smelled and looked and was quite changed. And then it all melted away and I was sitting instead in the library, which had been my father's 'Province', (as my mother termed it), where he lounged, and read books, and smoked cigars and drank brandy, and 'jawed' with male friends, and Eric, after dinner, far from the twittering of the women of the house.

Later, I met Elizabeth, the girl from the hall – which is curious because, when I saw her from the staircase that first time, she wasn't yet a ghost, nor fully grown up, and besides I seem to have gone farther back in time and place after seeing her, back to a *much* earlier period, perhaps only a few years after I actually died in 1918. Which is when I met Coral, and after that eventually all of them who were already here. But now, saying this, I'm not quite sure when I did meet each of them the first. Also, and I can't deny or explain this, I do feel in addition that I spent some time elsewhere. By which I mean I was somewhere that wasn't the house, though I have no notion where, but I wasn't unhappy there. It stays for me a mystery.

A memory – which I cannot remember. Haven't I said I am silly? What can we expect of me but an inadequate – what do they say? – *take* on events?

I apply that philosophy too to those awful things that have started to infest the landscape and the gardens. The Zomb-things, whatever they are. They frighten me so much. Once, one peered right in at a window on the ground floor, in the part that remains of the old dining room, and it pressed its broken nose to the glass, drooling. But Elizabeth came in and comforted me. Elizabeth is very kind, although sometimes she calls me 'Daphne'. This is because she once painted a picture, or made a statue of Daphne, from the Greek myth, as Daphne was turning into a laurel bush. I believe I have that correctly. Elizabeth said the Zomb couldn't see me, that it had neither a mind nor a soul. She reminded me I'd caught glimpses of such things in new-flickers on the

Tea V, before the pictures failed. And while she talked, it, the thing, wandered off.

Elizabeth called it Ugg, and made me laugh. She is smart and clever, what Constance used to say women should become. I wish I could somehow hold Elizabeth's hand for comfort. But none of us, alas, can touch, not a chair, not a tree, not each other. The last fleshly hand I remember holding, I'm afraid, is his, Captain Ashton's, who may not have been a captain at all. I don't know what happened to him. I don't even know his first name. Perhaps he died in the War. Or the other war that apparently followed. Or perhaps he lived. Whatever it was that he did, he went elsewhere. How sad this is. I have said enough.

4

Coral

Miss Archer murdered me. This is quite true. It is all I need to say.

Despite that fact, I would expect you will wish me to expound my claim, to provide evidence, and failing that, as how can I provide anything of such solidity, being murdered and dead, and, too, as constantly I was informed in my former life, I am only a child; failing that, as I say, I must argue my case.

I have no idea how I should do this. Nobody will believe me. The others here, all grown men and women, do not, I am sure. Nor will any other, nor you, whomsoever you are.

Certainly Miss Archer, who was, you understand, my governess, as they used to say in popular fiction, 'did me in'. I was 'done in'. I am done.

Now I shall start weeping again.

Miss Elizabeth says that a ghost can shed tears, it is allowed. She says she too has wept. Laurel, however, never weeps. Laurel is very strong and brave, a shining example to our weak feminine sex. My Father would have said that of Laurel. He had said that of my own lost mother. "How brave she was," he said. "Never a complaint. Her eyes released no single salty drop. A paragon among women." (I used once to believe a paragon was a bird, but it would seem it is not). "Take note, Coral," he would add, with his usual benign sternness, "of the bright example you must strive to follow."

"Yes, Papa," I would answer.

I was six when first he said this, and afterwards I was seven. I had lost her, you see, my mother, when I was a child of five years and nine months. Now I am fourteen. I have been fourteen for almost a century and a half. I have tried very hard to be what has been expected of me. And I have failed.

The situation that annoys me the most is that of my dolls. I had two that I was particularly fond of. And when I returned to my home after the rather curious experience I had following what I have to assume was my death, I found these dolls both propped up in one of the rooms, a room of display as I afterward learned. Supposedly it recreated a nursery of the time of our Queen, Victoria, although, to me, I confess, who spent her early years in just such a place, it was very unlike the original. However, seeing the dolls I ran towards them, to embrace them, my two wooden friends, that, I confess, I had retained into my fourteenth summer. Yet when I reached them I could not touch, let alone hold them. Of course not. I am a ghost. My hands passed straight through them. I wept then, again. Despite all my handsome and patient father's counsel, I never really could control my tears.

I had begun to cry on the day of my mother's funeral, when I was told I might not attend, for that would be unsuitable. Until then I did not think I had fully believed Mama had perished. My current nurse had told me gently, her own eyes wet, that Mama had gone to Heaven to be with God, and I railed against God, saying He did not need her as I did. My father, naturally, admonished me. After that hour, often, I wept.

The case of the dolls was worse in its way. My mother vanished from my life. But, returning, the dolls were and are here. It was some while before the consequences of my spectral state were confirmed and explained to me by Laurel, and later, Elizabeth. The old man in the library, once he became one of us, explained to me also, seeing I still chafe against my fate. He is a kind old man, and very clever. Everyone is clever save myself. But all of them lived longer than I. I was murdered before I had learned enough.

My Father was often away, and in the early days I had several nurses, who were gentle with me, and not strict, which was apparently a fault in them. No doubt their shortcomings added to my own. Yet I do remember comfortable times, such as eating hot buttered muffins by the nursery fire, and little games with puzzles, and a treacle sweet for a prize.

When I was just twelve, my father came back from half a year in another country, which I think lay on an enclosed sea called the Mediterranean. He found his house, he said, this venerable and significant building, erected in the 1600's on earlier foundations, and adjoining the historic ruined fortress that had stood on the site since 1289, to have everything unruly, and in a disgraceful condition of dusty untidyness and neglect. I, too, had been undusted and neglected, it seemed. He tested me all one long, greying afternoon, in his study, which room was very newly scoured and burnished, and chokingly perfumed with large amounts of lavendered beeswax, so I coughed continually, and my eyes ran, and presently my father upbraided me quite coldly for weeping again, when it was not the same thing at all.

During the interview otherwise, my Father learned my reading skills were poor, and I had attempted only worthless books, these being fairy tales and youthful romances, for children, of knights and such-like. Nor was my ability with simple mathematics of any value. He remarked I could not seem to add two and two, which actually I could, if not much else. What use would I be, he cried, if ever I should have to govern servants in my own husband's house? The poor fellow would be destitute in a week due to my ignorance. Nor had I luck with my embroidery, and my water-colours were undisciplined. It was not that he chided me, but more that I had clearly added to the general dissatisfaction he had. It seemed, for I had caught a snatch of below-stairs talk, the upkeep of the mansion was very costly, while his friends had dwindled in number sharply, owing to some failed business venture; which talk, inevitably, I did not coherently absorb.

The upshot was, however, he dismissed my nurse. Next a woman arrived, who was to be my governess.

Miss Archer, whose first name I learned once, by accident, to be Pomponia, a royal name from Ancient Rome, was extremely and frighteningly beautiful. And when first I glimpsed her on her arrival, my heart missed a beat, for she was like something from one of the tales I had read, instead of Thomas Carlyle's *The French Revolution*, or Plato's lectures.

Her shining hair was jet black, as dark as my father's own. Her eyes were a gleaming amber. All her features seemed to have a perfect shape, so that in whatever direction she turned, her face, from the front, above or below, or in either profile, astonished by its delicate flawlessness. Even her teeth were beautiful, and very white. And her complexion was like the petal of a pale flower. She had such pretty hands. I thought I should love her unreservedly. I did so. But also I feared her somewhat. Going to see her every day seemed to be like a visit to great royalty. She was always so gracious, and patient, but her beauty was distracting and – intractable. When she sang a song, trying to teach me the words and melody by this means, I could never quite achieve it, for to come in after her own presentation was onerous, a travesty.

Aside from this, however, a model discipline began to preside over my lessons. I was taught etiquette properly, and how to behave in company, although very seldom was there any, beyond the maid bringing cocoa at my bedtime, or my father sometimes joining Miss Archer and myself for the afternoon tea.

He and she spoke easily, despite her immaculate decorousness. Now and then he would discuss something with her at length, by which I mean he would tell her something, occasionally inviting her comments. This was unusual for him, I thought. I had not had the impression that generally he sought female confirmation, let alone advice, on any matter.

That winter there was a heavy snow. From upstairs, in my rather draughty bedroom, I could watch the white flakes falling and falling by the windows; while rising from the dining-room downstairs, through the vast snow-silence that came to enclose the house, I might hear her silvery voice singing at my mother's old piano, which Papa had finally had retuned. Or I might hear him laugh, in a different, warm and fireside way.

I wondered if, in the evenings, she ever told him ghost stories. She had once told one to me, and scared me, but she said sharply I must not be foolish. It was about an old man who haunted a house, he having powdered hair or wig, and he hated particularly all children, and murdered them with one terrible look of venom. Miss Archer said he walked an ancient and historic mansion, just like this one. I had many nightmares about him, but I was younger then. There is, on the other hand, supposed to be the ghost of a warrior from Ancient Times who haunts the ruined castle here, but I am never allowed in that part of the grounds, as once I caught a chill from sitting in the wet grass under the ruined tower. (But I never saw a ghost until I was dead.)

Despite my childish years and lack of knowledge, I believe I came to apprehend that the exquisite Miss Archer had fallen, soft and snow-like, and silent, somewhat in love with my father. It was like the noble romances in the books I had formerly read, before I had to tackle the works of duller, slower, more tedious and valuable writers.

Once, deep in a black freezing night, I heard her step in the corridor outside my bedroom. I thought she was coming to speak to me, which, once I had settled in my bed I had never known her do. But instead her quiet and dainty feet moved on along the passage, taking the corner towards the west wing of the house. At the time, sensationally, I wondered if Miss Archer were walking in her sleep. The western wing, certainly, had nothing in it to demand of her. My father's study, and other private rooms, lay there. Yes, you will mock me for my innocence. I recall even dear Elizabeth laughed when I told her this, so long after. But if anybody has been forced to wear a blindfold over one eye all their short life, how could they expect to recognise, even if so flamboyantly shown, what that one eye might see when uncovered?

One evening in the spring my father asked me to add my name to three legal papers. I did not know what they were, but once or twice had had to attend to such items before. I was not concerned. My task was soon done, and the papers meant nothing to me, were only to do with some little household matter that apparently my poor dead Mama had wanted left in my charge when I was twenty-one. I forgot the signing, as I forgot the others. I was struggling by then with an awful translation of a profound German novel, packed with precepts and exhortations and nobleness, construed in dark brown pits of untranslatably sunken prose. This was enough to dismay me. I needed no other worry.

We had a wet spring. I had gone out to look at the fruit trees in the orchard with the cook, who wanted me to mention to Miss Archer that she might tell my father some of the trees were sorely in need of attention. The cook had tried to pass this news to my father directly, but was not noticed, it seemed. Over the past five years all the gardeners had gone but one, an elderly, sottish man, who poached the nearby woods that, by now, belonged to another landowner. The result of some of the poachings came to our kitchen and were economically helpful, and so the man was not sacked for his otherwise laziness. Our funds were low. I had not been bothered, of course, as to how or why my father could or would engage such a governess for me as Miss Archer, when impoverished.

As the cook and I returned to the house, the rain came

down again, and both of us got a wetting.

Upstairs by the fire, Miss Archer found me drying my hair and grew abruptly anxious. "You should have more care, Coral. You know how very easily you take cold."

I was crestfallen to displease her. But by the hour of my supper, I felt I had incurred no harm. Miss Archer nevertheless did not agree.

"Oh, dear, Coral," she said, gazing at me with great attention, "you're pale and shivering. No, perhaps you don't yourself notice. We try to be brave, do we not, and to ignore these things? But I've known you quite some while, and I believe I detect the signs." She felt my forehead and my hands. "As I thought, your brow is hot, your fingers cold and clammy. You shall go up to bed at once, with a hot stone to warm you."

So off to bed I was packed, where I touched my own head and felt it, by then, quite hot, but that might be the fire, or the stone water-bottle. I hoped not to be ill. It was tiresome for me, and for my father, and the servants. The only ray of light in it might be not having to read any more of the unspeakable book.

Having eaten my supper, I lay back and watched the fire, and soon I fell asleep.

I have no idea what hour I woke, but by then the room was pitch dark and cold, and the stone hot-water-bottle stone cold. Before I could be concerned at how I felt, I heard again that delicate step in the corridor. I wondered if now Miss Archer would indeed slip gracefully into my room, to ask me how I did. Probably I wished she might. Although, maybe I am not entirely certain of that.

In any event, no other sound came, nor did anyone enter. I believed myself mistaken.

I was lapsing back into deep slumber, when something

occurred that I can only describe as being like a huge pale bird rushing down through the darkness, its gigantic wings feathering and creaking. And then it squashed home upon my face. A terrible and immoveable weight and power was behind it. Struggle and flail and churn about as I did, I was unable to dislodge it. I could smell damp and starch and dank cloth, and some other harsher smell, rather like metal, but not quite. But I had not been really awake, and those moments of semi-awareness were already being crushed from me like tiny sparks under the heel of a boot.

I was savage with panic and a surging horror such as I had never known, as vast chunks of nothingness crowded in on me. I had no single thought. I could not breathe, and as I choked and stifled, had the sense too of some other female life, also expunged in an oddly similar way, gasping and spasming, drowning; drowned. I believe, by now, this was a ghostly foresight of Laurel, who would die of the influenza plague, her lungs suffused by matter and fluid. In mine, if any had looked – which they did not – would only have been the nesty, tawny down of the very large pillow used to suffocate me.

What strength she had, Pomponia Archer, in her pretty little hands!

Because the others have spoken, and told me what they surmise, I can say the immediate medical verdict upon my death was, probably, that I had been the victim of a violent chill, caused by the rain storm, and my own foolish failure to change my garments. It appears, or rather does not appear at all, that those who are suffocated by the steadfast application of a pillow, or other impenetrable barrier, to the face, closing off the passages of breath through mouth and nose, very frequently display no evidence, save their heart failure, or, conceivably, a very rapid congestion comparable to a severe coriza. The story told of me by that evil woman must have been that I grew ill through the evening, refused any fuss, how bravely! – and died during the night of congestion, fever and a general weakness of my constitution, which was already evidenced by my other recurrent, if more minor, ailments. Doubtless she would have added that she would never forgive herself in being swayed by my reassurances. Perhaps she even pretended she had, after all, visited my room just before dawn, unable to rest herself in her anxiety about me, and so – alas! – discovered my poor little corpse.

My father would have credited the story immediately. He knew he had drilled me to be valiant, or as much as any mere female might be; to resist my own whimpering physical failings. Perhaps he was even proud of me a moment, even if my victory over self had led to my death. How often he has assured me my mother was "brave..." Never a complaint, even near death. "Her eyes released no single salty drop."

I must also admit I do not think he mourned me much at all, and then, his gorgeous mistress, Pomponia, was at hand to console him.

Why did she kill me? I have no definite conclusion, despite the time I have had to consider one. I think possibly only because I depressed her, in my unimportance, much as that weighty, highly-valued translated German tome had dragged down my own spirits. I was a set task for her that was, not merely unachievable, even for such a paragon as herself, but both intensely repellent and dull. I was therefore better closed and laid back on the shelf. In other words, dead.

My Prayer

After I died, I found myself in a long room, whose many windows were flooded by soft, clear light that did not dazzle, but neither was anything visible outside. I was on a bed, I thought. There were other beds, too.

At first some figures in long gowns seemed to pass to and fro, and I took them for women who nursed us. In the other beds seemed to be other figures. Then, gradually, as I came more and more to myself, I found nobody else was there, and the other beds were empty. Nothing in any of this disturbed me. I seemed to have been enjoying the sweetest rest, and now I was myself again, and I rose up, straight off the bed, and the light was warm and soft.

Aside from this very first memory, which still seems quite clear, any other things that happened for a time are blurred and I cannot remember them, certainly no details, only vague hints of colour, light and shade, or feelings – and the feelings were all pleasant ones, calm and happy. This is rather like a dream one had and then cannot recollect, only vague little scraps that drift and float away. And once, much later, I believe, I saw a man in an old-fashioned coat of green brocade, and dear Heaven how he scowled at me! But then he too was gone.

The next solid memory I have is of standing outside the nursery, upset it had altered, and not to find my dolls – although, as I have said, I did find them later somewhere else, and could not hold them any more. As I stood there, a young lady came along the corridor, in a dark blue costume, which shocked me slightly because it showed, quite clearly, her ankles, as only a young girl child showed hers. I particularly noted it, I think, since I myself had only just attained grown-up clothing. I have grown accustomed, obviously, to such hemlines by now. Even those of the later 'modern' women in the pictures, even Elizabeth's, which are only just below the knee; she has assured me that, when younger, she wore skirts even shorter!

Nevertheless, the young woman in blue stopped instantly and stared at me. "Are you here?" she asked. I said to her, "Yes, this is my home." And then she reached out, and her hand passed through my shoulder, and both of us sighed, knowing, even I, the reason. (This meeting is strange too, because it transpires Laurel died after I did. But then I might have lingered in that other place of light and unmemorised memories, and only come back here years after. I sense there was no true time there, in that place, no time as we know it here, alive, or dead. I could have returned at any moment. I am glad I did not do so while Miss Archer was still in residence.)

I pray for Laurel every evening, just after the sun sets. Awake during day or night, there seems no point in praying later, or by a bedside prior to unnecessary sleep. I pray for Elizabeth, too, and since he arrived, for the old man from the library. I never pray for the warrior from the 1300's. I can see him nowadays, of course, and I am shy of him, and he makes no proper sense to me when he speaks, although I wish him no ill, poor thing. Do I also pray for myself? I do not. My prayers for myself seem always to have been pointless.

Nor, naturally, do I ever bother to pray for them –

those others who sometimes invade our grounds. They are Monsters. One does not pray for a monster, only to be rid of it, yet that too seems useless. So many people must have prayed for that, and it has never worked.

There is some frightening joke I came to hear, in 'modern' times, that God had died. Perhaps He has.

Before the Tvie apparatus failed, as did the lamps Elizabeth and the old gentleman could somehow persuade to come on, I had already seen appalling images of the creatures, which we are to call Zom-bees.

If I had been only somewhat younger, and, of course, alive, I should have suffered horrible nightmares of them. I always hope they will go away as suddenly as they come, and leave no trace. But if one tide of them draws out, another high Zom-bee sea replaces it. In addition, now some of them do not go at all, but loiter around the grounds, occasionally stumbling and crashing against the doors and lower windows. So far only in two places did they gain access, and this, thank Providence, only in a part of the house none of us much visit; besides, it is becoming derelict. Nor did these Zom-bees linger indoors. They appear to prefer the open spaces, even if the weather is inclement. Yet, they do not make choices, surely, being entirely mindless. Every and anything they do, even should it appear to be, momentarily, evolved from a strategy, is merely accidental, a coincidence without meaning. They did not even eat the fruit they tore from the trees in the autumn. What they desire to eat is human flesh, or so the visions on the Tvie boxes showed us. There are no living humans here among us. And we have, as Elizabeth stresses, nothing to be alarmed at. Yet all of us, I think, are apprehensive.

The knight bears it worst, I believe. He will, as Laurel

has said, be used to meeting wicked violence with correction, and now, obviously enough, he cannot. But then, he will sit and watch Elizabeth for hours on end, or follow her about, a lean, noble and loyal dog, in chainmail, walking upright, and the wind not blowing nor the rain damping his long pale hair. He says very little. And when he speaks we do not understand him. Or, I do not. But then. I understand none of it.

The sun has gone. Everything is shadows. It is time for me to pray.

5

The Warrior

Then will I to tell of that I see in the efore,
  in my day of life, as when I am he that efore I am,
  as at this hour I am that now I am, and he another –
  for I am smoke and air,
  that am then the hot clay of created living Mann.

In the first I am of no wurth,
  and by two twelvemonth she that give me life does her
go with death.
  Amid churls and sad to nine years I am, likn the
worm, knows no thing.
  Crawler in dirts, so I.
  Then he is by. He that is my Lord.
  On that hour is he aged, so I am to think, of ten years
and six.
  On horse big as an house is he riden.
  Blac the hors, and he is of blac hair
  and eyen of him are dark,
  and likn the paur fol I gape, but he sees me
  and I think he say, but in a sort of words I am not full
to grasp, Him, then, paur him.
  And they takn me up but I am not cry, I am in lesson
by then to cry makn no altering.
  But too I am sworn to him in that hour, heartsure. And
gottn by him I am makn new.
  In whiles I am growen and learnd even somewhat to

scan words across a booke.

But most I am learnd to feight.

And so do I, for to be his man, to be among his husmen and guarde of him, a cnight.

As of then I am that you see me, and, when at war, a heaum on my head and scield by, and bladed sweord to hand.

One fine surcot for a feast, and one for battail.

The castel my haome, I that never efore has awhiht save mud or cauld or to be beatn with stick.

Averus, he I am is happy.

For elevn of years then I, and I then of twenty twelve-months, and he of seven and twenty such.

And I of his men, and feight by him, both in some smallr disputins and once, when my Lord is called to aid busyness of the King's own.

But my Lord is as my Father, or my brother.

Or he is, tho I must not say it, as my God.

For I have never seen the Christ, nor do the Christ ever touch me or talk to me, or sling his arm about me, nor give me his hand to kiss, nor speak so well of me after some blood feightn.

Nor does the Lord Jesu keep me in life, in food and shelterd, in despite of that the priest may say, so far as I may grasp it.

But my Lord Hroldar does so, and all and much and more.

Wyvmann I have too, girls to lay by me.

Sweet are all, but one very much.

But her babe that is mine come from her stilled. From which then she do not stay byen me. Such passes.

And he say to me then, Letn go, she.

But he gift her so she do not sofre more.

But we of his men, in peace days, we drinkn with him, and singen and meyri.

Like a sweord, a banner, he.

To follow him is to live.

I will not speak long of this.

There come about a querel betwn a neyhbour of powr and my Lord.

To castel then come these dogs.

It happen that efore, in the springn months when fever rise, fever takes me too. I was a great whiles sick

but by the hour the asseg begin I am myself hale again, and go to stand with my Lord on the rampart.

The foe many,but our stones strong. The grey time of the year too draws in, the cauld and dark.

They will weakn and slink onway.

But rather than such, one in our walls betrays my Lord Hroldar,

and by nightdark they in steal, our enemi.

A while that has not time we feytn. We are red from heel to heafd in flame and blood.

I by my Lord and one comes to murdr him

so I afore my Lord, and I strike true but aswill I takn the enemi blow.

Cloven I am and down I fall. But my lord lives through my act.

After then I hear a bell that rings, but then I go a whiles in shadow.

And when again I am in this place, others are here I never kno, nor myself they never see.

So it is I bide alone here, and would be no otherwhere.

My Lord Hroldar, though gone by my return, have then his life throu me, as I at first had gotn my tru life of him.

Averus, there is juste in this. I mak no querel.

The Enemi

There is the other enemi now at our gate.

They are uncumly and fuwl, nor menn, neither wyvmenn.

Things from out the old tales these.

I nevr see much and many creaturs but such as this never til this time.

Yet of the alterons of the castel, its ruiner and loss,

and the build then risn of the house,

such to me as ifn I clomb and stand aloft the wurld and gapen in at God-His jest.

Yet they that Eliseth names Sub-umbris

of Hell, they.

I would slay them everyone, but may not.

I am air now, and smoke.

When first I or my wraeth, that is all that is remained of me, see Eliseth,

I am takn one breath again of life.

As with my Lord, so she.

From her, my third life is.

Gottn of her, not wyvmon, nor Lord,

Never my modter, as never have I such a one save for unremembern.

My Cwene, Eliseth. My hlady. Forgivn mae I be, but will I not deny.

PART TWO

1

The Scholar

It was at Murchester, I recall, that some old duffer who, out of the kindness of his arrogant heart, (and fee aside) gave us a lecture on Keats – said lecture not in fact bad in itself – referred to that "plebeian phrase" which "enthuses" that someone or other is a "diamond". The old fascist proceeded, (nor did this either have much to do with the poet Keats), to instruct us that "among the ignorant, that inferior stone, the zircon, may be mistaken for a diamond," by such "morons" as did not "know diamonds very well." He was rewarded with a tepid scatter of laughter, none of it offered by me.

I have a reason for recounting this daft and spiky little memory, but I'll come to that.

When once we lost the visions of the TV and mental visions of the radio, (the world wide web was already gone, the first to fall in fact), along presently with the lights – a universal power *outage*, (as by then the more recent world was wont to call a power-cut or failure), our imaginations took over. We understood too that civilisation, at least inside the British Islands, had collapsed. Not much of a surprise, under the circumstances. And we were already, naturally, seeing on a regular basis the Zombie Hordes at our very doors, as it were, if in small numbers.

Elizabeth gives them names, the ones who hang

around now, while they do. What was it? Ugg and Jug –
oh, and Cog and Bog. There are a couple more names I
mislay. About ten or thirteen of the things congregate
here presently, I surmise, if rather irregularly. They are of
either gender, though males seem to predominate.

There was one evening I recall when El and I were
trying to see if we couldn't make the lights come on any
way by sheer telekinetic impulse: we could not; it seems
there has to be some electric power capability available to
start with, or no dice. But as we were giving up, there
came a sharp rapping on the French doors. It was one of
the 'modern' rooms, (added circa 1960), equipped in the
recent past with central heating and so on. Now in the
pitch black and chill – neither of which any more affected
us – she and I beheld a towering Zombie pressed against
the glass. Was it aware of us? We thought not. We were
not live flesh – *meat*. Some people can't see ghosts, as we
all realise, and some can, or they can see *certain* ghosts,
for some perhaps explicable but often unexplained
reason. This can work in reverse for ghosts as well. *They*
(we) don't always see living humans. Coral vows she has
never seen a non-deceased human since her death. Laurel
admits to having seen few, a then-living Elizabeth in her
teenage years being one of these. For our Knight, I'm not
sure either way. Probably Elizabeth knows his take on
things, for she's normally the only one he truly
communicates with, or who can half-way understand his
manner of talking. However, apparently, *all* of our party
can see the Zombies. Why is that? Because they *are* dead
even if still somewhat animate?

Elizabeth and I, without exchanging a word, went
forward to the glass doors. We could obviously pass
straight through them. But we did not. We stayed our

side of the window, and the Zombie stayed his, (it was indeed the remnant of a man, very tall and big-bodied, with a bald head and staring greenish eyes). He continued to knock.

Then finally the Zombie drew back, and raised his bulky fist to shatter the glass.

Mindlessly both El and I sprang away – though to us, of course, it could hardly matter. But something too checked the Zombie. It gave a strange swimmy squinty leer into the room, and turning suddenly, blundered off again. When it was about twenty paces away along the drive, it started a kind of ululating yodel. Now and then they do make sounds, presumably if their vocal chords are still intact. Sometimes they even *breathe*, or approximate hoarse breathing sounds, although one assumes their hearts no longer beat, and oxygen is as superfluous to them as to ourselves.

When the creature had blundered from our view, Elizabeth said, "A lot of them are almost intact, aren't they. I sometimes wonder what it must feel like – or do they feel anything?"

"Residually, one supposes, perhaps their *bodies* do, or with some of them that happens."

"I wonder if their memories remain, or any fragments of thought. Why else," she mused, "did it *knock* on the window?"

"Learned reflex, possibly. A merely physical reaction. No longer cognitive."

Then Coral appeared, asking anxiously if the "vile bee-thing" had gone.

Laurel was absent, as sometimes she is, leading her own lonely unlife elsewhere. The Knight was away, almost certainly making his nostalgic nightly patrol about the ruinous castle towers.

Tonight, just past midnight, which is usually when one can find all of us in the main body of the house, I mean to gather them together. I have had an idea. I have had it for about seven days and nights now, and have mulled it over. Part of me has even considered undertaking an experiment on behalf of this idea, privately and alone. But we five are a sort of club, aren't we? A Co-Operative. Which suggests to me I would be wrong to go ahead before at least outlining my thought to the rest.

We met in the 'new' sitting room, which was part of the most modern extras, a largish grey and red space, with small tables and big armchairs – on which, of course, we hardly ever 'sit', preferring to perch on the floor. Elizabeth has observed we manage not to sink through the ground outside, or the floors indoors, or the treads of the staircases, and says that we accomplish this by some unconscious effort of will provided us, perhaps, by a sense of pure logic, and that to sit on the floor is therefore less tiresome than to use the furniture. (We find, generally, even when we do make an extra effort and position our etheric selves on, say, a chair, once we take an interest in another matter, even in each other, we tend either to sink in – or, more ludicrous, float upward). (Irritating.) A TV stands against a crimson wall, a huge model from 2017, with a screen as wide, so it looks to me, as that old thing known as Cinemascope. But dead, now, a black blank.

I asked for everybody's attention, I'm afraid no doubt exactly as I was used to doing whenever I gave a talk at Murchester. A slight disquiet in me at broaching my idea had made me over-formal.

They listened politely, that is, the two girls did. The Knight listened only as if it were his duty to do so, standing rather than sitting just behind Elizabeth, her guard, her servant, her pale shadow. But Elizabeth, perhaps predictably, stared at me throughout, and when I stopped speaking, having said, I thought, what had occurred to me, in the clearest and most precise way I could, it was Elizabeth who broke out in a sort of astounded anger.

"Are you *mad*? Have you *gone* mad? Do ghosts *go* mad? *How* for Christ's sake can you suggest such a bloody disgusting *stupid* fucking *madness*?"

We, she and I, are the only two who did or still do swear or blaspheme. The girls, when we do it, used to look away, uncomfortable, (Laurel), or then look back, curious, (Coral), but that faded long ago. The warrior Knight seems not to notice particularly. Well, he was a soldier, he'll have heard plenty worse. Or else our modern usage fails to register with him.

"It isn't necessarily madness, El," I quietly said.

"It's crazy and disgusting. You're mad." Elizabeth let out her non-necessary breath in a fierce sigh. (How like *them* we are, are we not, the Zombies, in so many remaining ways?) "Why," she said, "did you dream that up?"

"It simply came to me. It seemed, once I'd thought of it, an obvious method."

She sprang to her feet and began to pace about, a restless lioness, pausing only once, to pass her hand reassuringly just above the top of the Knight's shoulder, saying only to him: "It's all right, I'm fine. Just annoyed."

I said, "Only think, Elizabeth, we'd be able to touch things again. *People* again. God knows, we might even start to breathe again. To eat and drink. *Sleep.*" I hesitated and lowered my eyes. "To kiss."

Coral too jumped up. She ran as if to Elizabeth, stopping midway and bursting into tears – those ghost tears that, despite what El avers, are dry, visible only in their sounds and gestures.

"She wants to hold her dolls," said Laurel, sadly.

"Perhaps, if we were able to do what I suggest we might try, she *could* hold them. Perhaps she would even be able to grow a little older, grow into womanhood."

Elizabeth rounded on me again, agitated and nearly smoking with rage. "Be *quiet*, old man. You don't know *everything*!"

"Who does?"

Then I noted El's Knight had lifted his head and was staring at me.

He spoke. I couldn't understand a word of the short sentence. But El turned sharply and stared in turn at him. "*What?*"

He repeated it, to my mind no more intelligibly. And then, far more expressive than this, he nodded to me, one brief positive nod – as if I had advised him of immediate battle, and he acknowledged and obeyed. And *then* his right hand rose and made over his mailed breast that beautiful and graceful sign, which still marks the believer's Cross of Christ. And stood after, his eyes no longer on Elizabeth, but only on me. Awaiting my order to advance.

And so I added, mildly, "After all, it may well be feasible to smarten up – how shall I say – our new habitations. Certainly they're not diamonds, but perhaps they can be zircons. A good zircon can fool a lot of people, particularly non-experts, that it *is* a diamond.

And they're still worth something. Zircons, Elizabeth. Still quite tough, harder definitely than air, and ghosts."

2

Elizabeth

I shouldn't have lost my temper. I don't dislike or disrespect the old man, our librarian.

Why did I?

Well, it revolted me. His *plan*.

And anyway it was absurd. It wouldn't work, how could it? No.

Thinking of it later, on and on, I did suspect rather I was also frightened gutless. Even without guts. And it is vile, too. I mean, given the state of them. My God. It would be worse than this aimless listless never-ending limbo. Wouldn't it? *Would* it?

To touch again?

To breathe and drink and sleep. And – love. To *make* love. Sex. But no, that wouldn't work, would it, either? Ha. Fucking ha. Even in the missionary position – Oops, there goes my left leg! And now the right – Darling, I've just accidentally bitten off your ear. Or, Darling, it just *fell* off, honest, when I hugged you. What's that on the floor? Ah, I knew I'd lose my head.

Of course, black humour aside, I'm thinking of him. My Knight in Shining Armour. I don't really know his name – something like *Gaume* is the way he seems to say it – Guillaume, perhaps. Who knows, now? Even his lord, the one he really loves, not necessarily in any sexual way, but heart and soul, my Knight says his name something like H.r.o.l.d.a.r. I have a feeling I've heard of this lord, Norman stock with some of the old Saxon mixed in, inevitably, by 1303 or whatever it was. Probably someone mentioned the lords of the castle-fort when I was here as a girl on that guided tour, and I heard the name then. It must be that. But the nearest *I* seem to come to the lordly name is Rauold, or Raul. It doesn't matter now, anyway. Rauold doesn't haunt here. Probably died of a surfeit of good living and bad wars, aged about forty-something, which tended to be the general rich and healthy extreme old-age-span back then, equivalent maybe to eighty-something now. And he went where most of the dead go, that mystery place that for some reason all of *us* didn't find, or couldn't.

I had to do a lot of translation and approximation on the Knight's story of his lost life, but I had a funny feeling, between you and me, that that last fight he had, and died in, is a bit – well, scrambled. Not quite what actually happened. It goes without saying it must be very hard to keep the facts straight if you die like that, the way the Knight did. Too sudden, too confused. Too terrible. (Not easy, as are pills and gin.) But I can normally sort of understand him, what he says. Not sure why. Because I fancy him, I suppose. It isn't love, though I care about him, and I feel affection... Let's not get too bogged down in all that. There's no way I can try to seduce him, not as we are. Unless, obviously, the Scholar is *right*.

But even if he is – I mean, to be *physical* like *that*? No. It couldn't work, or be any use.

Let me just explain, (to change the subject), about the translating I did on the Knight's story. It was very short, and that wasn't just me abridging or cutting corners. He has never said a lot about that, his life, death. Nor a lot about anything at all. (I've never grasped why women, the modern ones mostly, just after my 'Time', complained so much about men never talking. In my recollection, men frequently talked far too much. On and on. A quiet one, who only speaks when he has something to say, is a pleasant change. (I don't include my father in this. He spoke the right amount, not too much, never too little. Or if ever he did – well, I don't remember it).

To return to the translation-interpretation of the Knight, I tried to get it the best I could, and into reasonably contemporary English – what the Knight says isn't like that – while keeping (letting through) a bit of the flavour of its own phonetic and cultural essence. Which notion of mine really sounds up its own expletive deleted, doesn't it? I think actually I haven't done a very good job anyhow. My take on his words is both too obscure and too fundamental. But I did do my best. I don't think you'd have understood him at all if I hadn't – guided, shall I say? – the pen. Obviously, though, to avoid further confusion, he didn't use a pen to tell his story, nor a typewriter, let alone a word processor or computer. (I believe I'd have *loved* computers, if I'd lived long enough to experience them – though my damaged fingers might have been a nuisance. I didn't live long enough though, did I?) As for this general narrative, none of us wrote/write, type or tap anything down. None of us recorded or record anything. We can't *touch*, remember. Nor can we make an impression of sight or sound, normally, on the living. So how then is it you can take *any* of this dialogue of ours in – however you think you're receiving it?

The usual way. Some humans can't see ghosts, and

some can. Some can *hear* them too. Or can *pick up* what they are trying to communicate. And not everyone needs a Ouija board or other device. Some can just *do* it. So, QED, my unknown friend, you must have the 'Gift' as well, mustn't you? Sorry to scare the shit out of you if you hadn't realised. But there it is.

Putting all this out I am, evidently, procrastinating.

If I've shaken you up at all, I'm pretty shaky myself.

He – my Knight – *agreed* with the Scholar's plan. The only thing the Knight added to me afterwards was that thing he's mentioned before. He wants to take up arms against the horrible terrible sea of Zombies. Kill, *destroy* every one of them. As he is he can't, can't even blow in their ears. But if the Scholar's 'plan' could work – then the Knight will be enabled to invade and to slaughter as many as he wants. Which, of course, is a crucial anomaly in itself. But no word from him otherwise on finer points or anything. *My* silly momentary fantasy was of holding my Knight in my arms. Kissing his lips. His is to go back to bloody war. And win.

Can't blame him.

What now, then?

Well, first off I had to calm Coral down. She didn't understand what the Scholar proposed, or rather the *means* whereby it would be achieved (if it were possible). So Laurel, looking almost frozen with nausea, carefully explained. Then Coral became hysterical, a perfect Victorian-novel, text-book, dramatic overload, shrieks and non-wet tears – I'd never realised till then my tears must be non-wet too – and 'vapours'.

Once Coral had subsided, we all stayed there in the sheer lightless black room, through which we can all see with the most unflawed night-vision *never* allowed the living. Coral crouched and sobbed quietly, murmuring the names of her dolls, and Laurel sat like an image of snow, and *he*, my Knight, stood to formal attention, waiting for the signal that battle had truly begun. And I stood limply and thought of my dad, wondering what he would advise. And I felt the pain of his loss to me, fresh, the way it always returns, like a jackal tearing at a corpse, except this 'corpse' of mine isn't dead, can never be, it seems, fully dead. Like the tortures in the Greek hell or wherever it was. Rolling up the mountain a stone that never gets all the way, or Prometheus with the bird ripping at his liver on and on, for-liver-ever.

Fuck this. Why can't old men keep quiet?

3

Laurel

Perhaps because I am a fool, I could see what the librarian gentleman meant almost at once, and, too, I could see the potential solution that lay in it. Elizabeth was angry, but the Knight was in favour. Poor little Coral - how dreadful it must be to stay trapped at the age of fourteen years for – my stars, how long has it been for her? It seems it must be some one hundred and forty years or more. It has been unsuitable and sad enough to remain at eighteen, if only for rather more than a hundred. But now I felt a curious surge of – what was it? Hope.

It's but too plain how many disadvantages there would or might be, but perhaps there will also be some way of evading these, or adjusting or tidying them, so that they become bearable, while our present state, really, isn't bearable at all. Besides, if the whole enterprise proved too vile, could we not escape it again? Of course I'm unsure of that. As of so much. I would have liked to question the scholarly man, but was overcome, as so frequently, by my shyness, and the sense I have, even now, that almost everyone else is probably in the right, except myself.

I am trying now to compose myself, yet my heart – no longer real, but only metaphorical – leaps and dances about.

(I have some concern about myself too. Can a ghost go

mad? Some two or three minutes ago, I believed I saw another old man, with strange grey curls, standing out by the house wall. He had a sorrowful and angry face. But no sooner did I see him than he was gone. I must have imagined this. Yet why I should eludes me. But even so I draw from it an unfavourable opinion of my remaining wits).

To live again, in whatever manner, must be more healthful than this. Surely, surely, we should try?

But the Scholar has gone up again to his library. All of them, even I, tend to keep very much to our own certain parts of the house. Therefore now I stand alone at an upper window, and look out across the moonlit grounds of what, once, was my unwarm and friendless home. I think of my mother screaming, in grief or petulance at my loss, perhaps in guilt, although I doubt she ever supposed she'd been unfair to me, or negligent. I think of Captain Ashton.

Then, far down among the savage shrubbery and the long-clawed orchard, not any fantasy but decidedly present, one of the sub-creatures emerges, and goes shouldering and staggering on its ghastly way. Yet now, absurdly or sensibly, I don't know why, or which, I stare at it and decide that it is only the thing's utter lack of motive and inner guidance that make it both so clumsy and so cumbersome, indeed so gratuitously repellent. Like a carriage running downhill without horse or driver, or one of those automobiles, also made driverless, its engine running on a directionless power, not knowing left from right, nor right from wrong.

4

Coral

I want my Mama. I want her. I don't remember her, but I want her. Where is she? If I am here, why is she not here? When I died, after Miss Archer killed me, why did not my mother come to hold me, and lead me through? Or... Lord Jesus, as we were promised? Where were they? My mother and God. Nobody loved me enough. And so, I lost my way. I am here. I am here, and I have no one to care for me, and the old gentleman has gone quite mad, as Elizabeth said, and he wants her to do this thing I do not understand with the Zom-bees. And I am afraid! I want my mother! I want my dolls! I want not to be dead! I am crying now. Can you hear? My tears are wet to me, but not to any other. I cannot even have my tears. I cannot show them. My Father would approve of that – not one salty drop! He must have cursed me.

5

The Warrior

(Completely interpreted by Elizabeth): I am of a mind with
the old man. Here is the way and the means. Into our
hand our foe may be delivered. We have been chosen
from the ranks, or otherwise, yet it falls to us. We will
enter them, as air enters in at the mouth and nostrils of a
man, or light at his open eyes. As that is, so we shall be,
for we are smoke and air, and they, the Monstrous
Enemy, are open jars of flesh that we may penetrate,
invade and fill, and kill them there, and rule there, and
be, and live, kings and queens, again each in our own
House of Body, under the Will of God. In truth I vow.

PART THREE

1

The Scholar

I had my eye on one for four or five days. Ever since I had thought up that extravagant and possibly impossible idea of mine over the course of a week. Most recently I had gone from window to window, upstairs or down, following this chap, (a male Zombie, another who had lingered here), to watch him. To *study* him. I did not inform the others of this. Before, or since. The ones of our number who seemed or were appalled, and adamantly hostile, who when, initially, I spoke to them, (El, Coral? Laurel..?), might lose their cool, (as they used to say), entirely. While our Knight might just lose his head and leap into premature action. A warrior unable to fight, as his training and living life had educated him to do, for over eight centuries, must be gagging for a 'bloody good brawl'. Caution, therefore. But the morning after our 'discussion' in the red and grey room, I moved out through a window into the grounds, to see if I could find my quarry, and take a look at him closely.

The reason he particularly caught my attention, I suspect, was his – by now rather faint – likeness to myself. Oh, not that he was my double – hardly. But he was of, shall I say, the same apparent type. Tall, six feet and a bit more, thin but with a solid, big-boned frame. In age he had been fifty or so, some forty years my junior, when struck down by the Zombie sickness, and emptied of his life-force and/or soul. Nor did he have the strong head of hair I had mostly managed to retain. All his teeth that I could see, however, (now and then he was prone to bare them in a snarl at nothing – or everything), were present. There did seem to be some damage to his right arm; it hung rather imperfectly. Perhaps it had been broken and not set. Not, of course, a favourable attribute for my purpose. Although conversely I had noted he could still move the *fingers* of his right hand. His left arm and hand, and both legs, were fine. His torso had taken some bashings, or else suffered some slight amount of decay, but none of this was either spectacular or especially gross. His eyes and other features were, like his whitish teeth, seemingly intact. Obviously he moved in the usual blundering, incoherent manner. But that, I thought, was due solely to his condition of cerebral void and absent reasoning.

The weather was raw but bright, with a snappy wind raking over the trees, shaking the orchards, and the woods below, their branches and buds, like the sistra of Ancient Egyptian temples. It is late spring, I think. I haven't mentioned this before, but then again, and given our state, we are all prone to this; seasons seem to last for a year or more, or vanish away in a night. One day spring, the next deep winter. Perhaps that really happens, at least from our perspective. Again, I recall the constant alarum of the 1990's and 20-teens about Global Warming and climate change... I seem to recall a ship went out to the Antarctic a few years following my physical demise. It had been sent to monitor the environment, and to prove thereby that the great ice-sheets were melting away. Instead it was stuck for days – or was it weeks? – in solid, unnegotiably-frozen ice. The relevant scientists hastily assured the world that this solid ice was actually yet further proof of dangerous climate change... contrary to appearances. I myself, I remember, believed that if our planet was warming up, it was due certainly in part to the earth's preparation for a new approaching Ice Age, even if said event was millennia in the future. (A little like turning up the central heating to combat a forecast snow-in, and to stop the water-pipes completely freezing.) In any case, no doubt the total loss of all light, heat, and electronic communication, recently, will reduce humanity's vauntedly pernicious evacuations of carbon. Though God knows what the nuclear power stations, and other such piles, will do, untended by humans, and/or broken into by the Zombie-kind.

I wasn't thinking of this, I always try not to, when I began to stalk the particular Zombie I had selected – if 'stalk' is the word: he was my goal...my what? Target? *Prey*?

He was seemingly quite unaware of me, as he lurched along, occasionally veering in among the wilded trees. A rushing lorry without a driver, a plane in full flight without a pilot – that was the impression I had of him.

I cruised along behind him, sometimes less than three feet away. Despite being dead, and mostly unable to smell things, as unable to touch or eat, I still became convinced I could detect his stink. But it was the reek of an unwashed and mobile body, I thought, with no true hint of rot or gangrene. Yet something there was. Something rank beyond mere human functions which, anyway, one assumes, occur with Zombies but infrequently. (Although these things devour living fleshly men and women, the Zombies do not appear to open their bowels or bladders, or if they do, the results have not been either witnessed, or whiffed, by myself). I have never thought to ask my fellow ghosts.

Finally my 'quarry', if I can call him that, appeared to stumble over something and thumped down on his face. I rushed to his side. I was concerned only that he had not been further damaged. But he made no vocal noise, neither of shock or pain. Well, naturally not. Everyone was assured his kind did not any longer feel such things.

However, as he lay in the thickening grasses, he rolled a little, and for a second his mindless eyes met mine. Did he see me? No. Yet, I calculated, maybe something in him, that which was left of what, once, his brain had been, perhaps *that* did. Since a look, part bewilderment, part fear, slid across his face. Did I, I wondered, imagine this? Before I could form an opinion, he slithered round, apparently unimpaired, even his broken arm not more broken, and bumbled to his feet.

He neither ran nor crept away. He was as before, a cerebral orphan, shambling off along the slope. I let him go.

And then it came to me. At which my own shock was such I believe, if I had been live flesh, I too would have fallen. But instead I simply lost contact with the .ground, and floated for a minute, levitating weightlessly.

For something too had happened to me. When he had fallen over – and he *fell* – a split second – no more –

That look of fright and confusion that had flicked in and out of his eyes, my God, it had been *mine*, or rather the *echo* of mine. For now I grasped I had, in the split second *preceding* the first, seen through his eyes the *other* way. That is, I had looked *out of him*, out of his head, his brain, his skull. And I had seen – not him, prone upon the ground – but landscape, trees and a misty vapour that hung in air, and somewhat resembled... the shape of a tall old man, whose likeness definitely I, in earlier years, (in mirrors, photographs), had beheld before: my own.

Myself. Through the eyes of the dead Zombie I had seen *me*.

That night I called them together again, there in the TV room.

"I believe it can be done," I said. "I believe, if only for a second or two, I have already accomplished it."

They sat in silence.

Like the set of a play, or movie, they were, as before, almost all seated, only the Knight standing. Their eyes, that seem to me three dimensional, bright and solid as those of physically living things, had fixed and now stayed on me.

Then Coral started tearlessly to sob, and Laurel sadly stretched out her hand to Coral, but could not touch, and Elizabeth uttered an obscenity under her non-breathing breath. The Knight quietly stood to attention: he was listening to a briefing in the War Room.

"I shall try the move again," I said. "I'm quite prepared to do it tonight. The Zombie I've been watching is in the orchard again. Most of the others are elsewhere. There is a chance," I added, I admit with some internal misgiving, for to say it aloud to them seemed to emphasise an unease I'd been trying to refuse myself, "a *chance*, once properly in, I may – how shall I say? *Get stuck*."

"You mean you'll rush in to that filthy body and become trapped," said Elizabeth. Her voice was cold as the Antarctic ice I mentioned, that itself *trapped* the research ship six, seven years ago.

"Yes, I do mean that. To enter with total intent could be irreparable."

"Then, if you can't get out, what do you think will happen to you?"

"I have no proper notion. I may go insane, I mean my awareness may. The Zombies are mind-dead, if not brain-dead. They can't reason, or seem not able to do so. That could be as infectious to an intruding life-force as the Zombie-plague was – is – to living tissue."

"Then you're a damn fool, aren't you, to try it?"

"Maybe."

"No maybe."

"I was there a moment today. Or so it seemed. I think I'm not damaged."

"You escaped."

"No, El. I didn't escape. I – fell out again, exactly like someone sliding carelessly out of a window. I must have fallen *in* the same way. But I'm guessing that even happened because I was *planning* to do it, if not consciously concentrating yet. Mind literally over matter."

"This is shit."

I said nothing.

Nobody else did either. Coral had stopped sobbing. She was pleating her ghostly skirts, or thought she was, over and over, in one hand. Laurel was watching me, oddly impervious; I couldn't tell now if she were sternly averse or vaguely intrigued. The Knight, I assumed, waited only for the Cry to Arms.

"I'm going out then, in ten minutes," I firmly said. "Does anyone want to come too? Not for you to do anything particularly, you understand, I don't expect participation, let alone rescue if it all goes wrong. But if you just might want to watch and learn, and see what happens next."

2

Elizabeth

I don't believe what he told us just now. I think he believes it. He imagined it, it was a fantasy – what my father used to call, so kindly, 'Imagination Pictures' – pictures, or movies, that is in the sense of films. He used to call it that when I told him of my prolonged waking dreams of playing piano concertos to a huge audience, or falling in love with handsome heroes out of history, who then carried me off.

And we ghosts can imagine things even now, can't we? We even imagine our bloody tears are still wet.

3

Laurel

I do believe him, the Scholar. Yes, that was what firstly
alarmed, and then made me wander about in a worse
daze than usual. And then see old men in brocade coats! I
think I shall follow the Scholar, as he suggested, but
keeping back a little, not to impede or distract him. Then
– well, we'll see, won't we?

Probably very foolishly I keep asking myself now, if
his gambit does work, how shall I then choose – the
librarian has already chosen – whom I should pick for my
new... residence?

But however could I select from among these awful
remnants – these things. To be frank, I would have great
trouble, when alive, in choosing which dress or hat I
would put on, hesitating over how suitable it was, how
often I had recently worn it, if it helped in any way to
minimise my un-attractions. While for dances, or parties
at the house, my Mother, or Constance, or both together,
would exasperatedly advise and guide me, as ever, with
new clothes: "Oh, now, Laurel. Not that mauve. No, no, it
will make your complexion even more pasty."

"Oh, how funny you are, Loll–" this being Constance's
sometime-abbreviation of my hedgerow name – "you
must never wear green, dear! Your eyes will simply lose
all colour. And you'll look quite bilious. Make everyone
else so, too!"

In this way, we see I'm unfit to make a proper choice. And especially since the material I must now choose from is extremely suspect.

4

Coral

I will not. I will not. I will not. Never will I. Oh – my father would think me even more vile. He would make use of that name he used, and which I overheard, so playfully then to Miss Archer, though to her he meant no harm, I am sure. A whoore.

5

The Warrior

I shall walk at his back, the wise and valiant old man.
Already, from attending on him, my mean of language is,
to my thought, of better clearness. My Eliseth could not
entrain me in this. But there. She is a woman. And it is
that I am ever learned in any matter by my own kind,
men. I would die to serve my lady. But my slowen mind
can not, of she, nor the female race, gage any teaching but
little.

Then so, I to hind, will watch on him, and what he
may do.

And if he is able, then I too, as have he, will seek and
make choisn, and accomplis all.

PART FOUR

Gravely Embracing

(*The Scholar*): As I went out again into the grounds of the house, I believe my mind, anxious and over-excited at my task, began to indulge in – not precisely displacement activity – but a sort of displacement thinking. Roughly or exactly, I was working out, dependent on my knowledge of them, my approximate age at the time of each of my fellow ghosts' deaths. (Obviously, this did not apply in either Coral, or the Knight's case. He certainly had out-deathed us all, centuries before any of us were born).

When El died, around 1974 or 5, I had been fifty-eight – sixty. When Laurel died in 1918 – I was a boy of three or four. As for Coral, I had deduced her exit occurred in the 1870's. I then arrived on earth some thirty-six to forty-six years after she left it. Have I pointed out I am, rather ridiculously, the oldest in age among them, but the youngest in ghosthood? An elderly baby, full of infantile newness, needs, and teenage solutions.

Once a church bell could sometimes be heard ringing from the church still standing a few miles off below the upland. But by 2012 it was no longer rung, and by now, naturally, no one attends the church at all. Oddly though, tonight, I seemed to sense its musical if tinny notes. I knew that the darkness had circled round to three in the morning.

No moon, but the stars, unpolluted by lights, were brilliant as faceted, true diamonds, some of them even showing their colour tints, yellowish or palest blue, and there a tawny one, the eye of a fierce, space-hunting wolf.

He – my 'prey' – was nowhere to be seen.

This seemed ominously apt. I had screwed my courage to the sticking place – and my 'victim' had skived off.

Someone was behind me, also, walking almost in my footsteps. The Knight. I had expected him, and there he was. We did not exchange even a single incoherent word.

In the end I reached a break in the fruit trees. Now and then, even at night, one might find rabbits or hares feeding on elements in the grass. I did not know as a rule what they identified as food, but generally my presence did not disturb them, although many of their number seemed to sense me. Inevitably, a Zombie presence scared most or all of them from the vicinity. Tonight, no hares or rabbits.

I looked out from the trees, away towards the ruined fields, down to where a village had once been. (I gather it was more or less deserted by the early 1950's, having been twice emptied of young men by two world wars.) A strange phenomenon was in the air, which occasionally I had noted before. Where the view was open, and the sky open too, ripples of thin light seemed wavering down from the stars, filmy silvery ribbons. How beautiful this world is, despite all its horrors and injustices. How can we bear, given any choice, to leave?

Then, only then, (I read something, no doubt superstitiously, into this), *My* Zombie, for want of better words, lurched forth into the benighted morning.

He was coming up the hill, hurrying even, in the strangest way as if, pardon my elderly infantile take on this – as if he was aware he was late for our rendezvous.

I braced myself. I drew in a huge and non-actual breath.

And then I fired my will, my essence, my ghost, like liquid lead from some appalling cannon, outward, forward, directly at him.

We fell as one. It took me some while to accept why. We had fallen as one – since now – one amalgamated Thing we were, he and I. I had done as I meant to, and entered into him. In his body, flesh, blood, brain – and I was him. He was – I.

(*Elizabeth*): Somehow, through the thick wall of night, I felt it happen. Or that was only some hysterical nonsense left over in me.

But it was like a deep, subsonic *boom*. Unheard yet *absolute*.

I thought, Christ, that stupid old man has –

I thought, Oh God, librarian, are you all right?

The very ground seemed to shift – no, not like that absurd analogy for sex. (The earth *doesn't* move when you come. You do, *we* do. We erupt from our ecstatic bodies in a fit of bliss and refound connection to *everything*. *We* move. The earth remains our shelter and our lover and mother, and kindly watches us as we hit the sky, then fall, gentle as silver ribbons, back into her arms. *There*, she says to us, sweet and low, *well done. Now you know the truth, my baby.* But of course, God help us, we forget.)

(*Laurel*): Treading behind the Knight, I believe neither he nor the old man noted me. My common lot always! But for once, perhaps, helpful.

I saw everything that happened, and was duly terrified, when the librarian and the creature fell, flailing, in a sort of collision, both of them, limbs and motion. Generally I don't see the others, (nor myself, those parts of myself I am able to see, for mirrors do not reflect us), as anything other than solid. But the old man became at first translucent, then transparent, and so disappeared. It seemed to me then the monster had swallowed him up, absorbed and killed the last living filaments of him. Yet then – then – the Zom-thing rose again to its feet. And as it was standing there, I saw in it a just discernible difference. How it stood was more coherent, less haphazard. How it turned its head, which all at once no longer seemed that of a disjointed doll. And it spoke. Or its voice spoke. Although its words were incomprehensible, and drool ran from its lips, yet they somehow conveyed to me a sense of triumph. But was this the triumph of the creature, having destroyed the librarian? Or of the librarian, who truly had, maybe, possessed it?

Then, feeling the dribble on its chin, which surely never before in its zomboid state it would have done, it lifted up its right arm to wipe its mouth.

There was an awful crack, huge in the still cold air, a noise as if someone had snapped a thick strong twig.

And the thing bent over, clutching at its right arm with the left, and cursing, for I could make out parts of the oaths more clearly than I had the few words of speech.

The Knight ran forward however, and he flung his own arm about the reeling creature to support it – and of course, the Knight's ghost arm passed right through the physical body of it.

After which we stood, all three – or four? – turned to a kind of stone with alarm and amazement. And all our quartet of paralysed, unasked and unanswered questions falling round us, like a glittering shower of winter snow.

(*Coral*): From a window, high up, I saw. I do not know what really happened. Now I am crouching below the window-sill, on the floor. The old gentleman has gone. We have lost him. Where is Elizabeth? In a minute I will collect myself and run to find her. What else is there to do?

(*The Warrior*): Himself he have gained his victory. So I credit. I stay to wait on him, for though his face now is that of another man, yet now that same seems full manlike, as before this creature was never.

(*The Scholar*): When the Second World War began I was in my early twenties; I'd been a small child during the 1914-18 rumpus, in the course of which, evidently, my father had died. We had never been well off, although my mother, certainly, came of what then was reckoned a 'genteel' family. She was magnificent, that lady, at concealing from us both, myself and Edward – Eddy – my younger sibling – he born some five months after our father's death in France – that her heart had been broken. But inevitably I must conclude that Eddy's death smashed any healing of her heart that he, and I, had been able to achieve. After her death, I was foisted on various relatives – cousins, once a diabolical aunt known as Sissy, (whom I called "Hissy" in secret). Luckily I managed well at school despite the rest, and finally won my place, if not at Oxford or Cambridge, in Murchester. That town, with its own charmingly dreaming spires, became my family. I learned and grew there, and much later went back to work in the magnificent university library. Until ousted at age seventy.

But to return to my starting theme. I was around twenty-four or five at the outbreak, (as they were pleased to call it), of the second major war. I was even then at Murchester, although I had also done some travelling through Europe, writing essays on my sojourns in Rome, Paris, Athens and Vienna. I seem to have been largely oblivious, possibly due to personally-benign unawareness, of the rising tides of power-hunger and Fascism. To start with I, like others, thought – or hoped – no war would occur. When it did I carried on, like countless thousands of others, head firmly cemented in the sand. However, time and evil marched on, and in the end it seemed I should be *called up* – extraordinary phrase. Called up like the dead, I suppose, from my inertia and cowardice. I did not, needless to say, wish to go. The programme of Army Life and 'Discipline' horrified me far more, I have to admit, than the notion of killing, or being killed. I did not besides think I could die, at first, which may only have been the euphoria of youth. But I began to be haunted by dreams of my father's death, mown down on a murderous shore, and also of Eddy's death, howling at first in agony, and then sedated to a corpse – even through both these events had been somewhat concealed from me at the time.

An old tale: a friend at Murchester pulled some strings for me. I had to leave my intellectual work, but ended with a war-assisting desk-job in London. The bombing there was such that I, along with others I met, partly believed I would have been safer as a soldier, out of

England and in the Thick of It. God knows.

But here now we come to the salient point. We come to the reason for my new digression. We come to the thing I had (resolutely no doubt) 'forgotten' all those long, long, long years after, when once peace gloriously returned amid the blasted shells of bombsites, rationing, sad dark gallows humour and inane optimism, that marked the late 1940's and early 1950's, when I was thirty/thirty-five going on ninety-six.

It was back in the Blitz night of a particular air raid; I have, now, no idea which or even the exact date – a penalty, one sees, for trying to wipe such memorabilia from the brain forever.

I was somewhere near The Strand in London, having been lured out by a group of others at the office for an elicit steak of horsemeat, or some such.

When the sirens went, (Sirens! Wails such as Odysseus never heard–), I took off for cover in a shelter near Clamber Row, and was going fast, when I met a man in uniform. A soldier.

He was young, probably about two years younger than me, I being then around twenty-six or seven.

He wanted a light for his cigarette, I recall, and we huddled in the lea of some huge old stone monolith of a building, while a match was struck – no matter the light, the enemy was already at work illuminating everything, and needing no extras from the citizens, for half the city it looked was blazing with bomb-bonfires. The sky was the colour of a blood-soaked pillow, lit up inside by cores of orange. The city itself otherwise looked already like a necropolis, the stony buildings dead, grey and hollow, empty of any living thing, yet glimmering with red stagelight from the incendiary rain. Now and then one of the deadly things came down, now far away, now nearer. It was like a storm, where the thunder and the lightning had married – a crash and flash, a purple blank, the scarlet aftershock, the roar and rush of gold and blood. And between each major concussion, a sort of silence, filled with roaring and emergency bells and cries and steep collapsing bellows and sighings.

"Busy night," he said, as we shared his cigarette – all mine were gone – against the wall. "I tell you, it's safer where I was, and where I'll be again, day after tomorrow. You shoulda joined up, Sonny."

I said nothing. It was a very odd thing. Our shelter, stone and darkness flimsy as tissue paper, seemed safe for now. As if we had, he and I, entered some integral pocket of space and time, just off the map of existence.

"Why didn't you then, eh?"

"Why – didn't I–?"

"Join up, Son. Look at you. Strong young toff like you. You're about my age, ain't yer? Bit younger? So what was it? Too scared?"

We were close under the so-wreckable overhanging portico, against the tissue-paper tomb wall. In the matchlight, and now in the black redness, I could see his face. A beautiful face, in its own way, with big narrowed eyes, now dark, now pale, as the bomb-light lit them.

"I don't know," I said.

"Don't yer? Well I do. You're a bloody coward. Still. Never mind. You're my type, you are. I don't like the girls, you see," he said, and I shuddered at it. But then he reached out and took my penis and balls into his big warm silent hand. And leaning in, he kissed me.

Nothing like that, ever before. Though, if I am honest,

hints of it in dreams.

I won't describe that moment. Please understand, I am not ashamed of it. In my subsequent life I saw and learned a lot. There was no wrong in my feelings. Only in what came next.

Because, before any proper action could ensue, I pushed him off. And such was my false and mindless panic, I managed to thrust him off balance too. In my own way I was physically quite strong, I must think, if mentally a weakling. He skidded back and hit his head against the nearness of the wall. I imagine he had been drinking, too. And so had I, to wash down the horsemeat and the expense of the bill, most of which had been allotted to me to pay.

As he let me go I turned and ran away. He lay on the ground, not knocked out, simply rather stunned, by the wall, and by my refusal – plainly my body at least had evidenced willingness. My stupidity must have been to him a kick in the guts.

Not until I had reached the turn to the next street did I look back to see him thus, lying there, laughing by then, rueful and – innocent. That beautiful and lost soldier, doubtless two years my junior, as my poor brother had been, not yet twenty-five...

If I hadn't pushed him off, if the wall hadn't momentarily stunned him, if he had been more sober, and I more self- aware.

The bomb however was eager, and had greater knowledge than either of us. It swung from the sky like a gigantic black-blazing wing, noiseless – or so thunderous it deafened me. It struck the place where we had stood, and where by then, laughing, he lay. The street exploded into splinters of volcanic fire.

It would have been both of us, if I had given in to myself. But I had not. So it was only him.Why do I, fool that I am still, reckon if we had been together, screwing into each other against the tomb-tissue, that bomb would not – would not – have fallen where it did–?

Before him, never, and after him, never. Not for me. I have never known love of the body. Never fucked. But in my own fashion, I have facilitated murder. If he had never seen me, chances were he would himself have made it to a shelter. Or he would have been a street or so away. Or if I had remained, and the bomb had dropped, ultimate orgasm. No *petite mort* but *grosse mort*. Death with death.

And until this moment, *this* moment – I had wiped it off my mind. But now, now I remember.

(*Elizabeth*): I know he made it work. The Scholar.

He meant to and he did.

I *felt* it, how he lunged and leapt and passed inside the body of the Zombie. And became a part of it. Did he then lose himself? I don't think it was that. Although I don't know.

Can't know.

Until I do it too, I won't.

But I'll *never* do *that*, will I, for God's sake?

Never.

Along the passage I came across Coral, poor little thing, crouching under the window in her formal Victorian dress. She wasn't crying, but she turned up to me her terrified little face. Poor kid.

"I saw," she said. "Through the window. The old man

sprang – and *vanished* into the bee-thing. Oh! Oh!"

I would have taken her in my arms, but we can't, of course. We can't cuddle or console or embrace or touch or properly weep.

"I saw it, too," I said to her, as levelly as I could.

I had, you see, hadn't I, in my own way, inside my ghost's mind "Do you know, Coral, I think he'll be fine." She said nothing, shuddering as she crouched on the floor, holding her own self in both arms. (I suppose we were always left with that. We can touch ourselves. Or seem to. But really, too, I wonder sometimes if we only *believe* we can. An hallucination of the embodiment ripped from us at death...) "I bet," I said, trying not to sound too confident, which I was not at all, anyway, "I bet our librarian will make it right. Let's hope so. Then he can give the horrible thing a bath, and make it start to talk again, and then he can tell us, through its mouth, if this was a good idea, or a bad one."

Coral stared at me.

She said, wary and cold, "Will *you* do it, too? Try to *go inside* one of them?"

"Certainly not, darling," I said. "Yuk."

She smiled warily when I said "Yuk". She's always seemed to like that dopey but so-descriptive word. I'd hoped she'd smile. And I smiled too. I said, "Let's go and see if we can find the others."

Inwardly, obviously, I wasn't smiling.

My mind was still rushing after the Scholar, what he had done, its unmatched sequels –

Because of course I knew this lady, me, was protesting too much. If that old gent could do it, Elizabeth was going to do it too. It was the only chance.

And the very thought of that made me, as our

American friends, with their often perfect use of language, used to say: sick to my stomach.

(*Laurel*): It seems the arm of the creature had been broken – or the bone dislocated. The abrupt gesture it had just now made of wiping off spittle – because the librarian made it – must have snapped the bone back into place. The clever librarian told us this presently, the Knight and I, and by then, although the new mouth he used still somewhat slurred the words, I could understand everything he said. It was even rather like his voice, as we knew it from his ghost, only slightly altered by the other's throat. For of course he spoke through the creature. Except, it seems, it's not a creature now. It is re-becoming a man, becoming the librarian. But there was some mood too that suddenly came over the old man next, and he turned from us and limped – then walked, a little way off. He stood by a tree, or he made the body do so, and he inside it. He was able therefore to lean on the tree, which also, in a while, he told us was pleasant to do. He didn't tell us what the mood of trouble had been, apart from the pain in his arm. Perhaps the mood was from some memory of his previous life, the life before he became a ghost, started all at once by becoming flesh again. But tears ran down his face. I saw them in the glassy clarity of the starlight, and they glistened, and were so wet.

I have seen her in a glade. As the Scholar did, I think, I looked for and found her before my mind was completely made up. I'd been watching, yet partly not aware what I was at. How we hide things, both ghosts and the living, from our own selves!

Morning was coming, the sky coloured like the pale white wine I've seen in fine crystal goblets in this very house, so very long ago. And there she sat. There's a tiny thread of fresh water that comes there out of a rock into a pool. The pool is full of rotted fallen leaves and less natural mess, but the rill is pure. I don't remember such a waterfall in my own past. They must have found it since. But it's always possible, it seems, to find, and to refind. It falls like clean tears. It's wet. And here then I may, if I achieve entry into her thin little body, and take charge of her as the Scholar has of the other one, wash her clean of the dirt she's coated in.

How old is this woman? Older than I, for sure. I died at eighteen years, and as a remnant of myself have so remained eighteen. But her body, I suppose, is past its first quarter century, twenty-five years and a little more.

Her hair, though thick with filth, and, perhaps, old blood, is palest yellow. And this not from some bleach or dye, but her own true colour. Her eyes are grey, like mine, if a touch darker. She was, and has stayed, strong. Just two fingers missing, the last two upon her left hand. Presumably, if I can master – or become – or dwell inside her, I can manage without them. An old wound has healed in her right side. The scar is like one a warrior might bear. If he weren't a ghost, but live flesh still.

As I approach her, she raises her head and looks at me. Then she stands up and makes a sound. I'm not certain if this frightens me, but even if it does, I won't be stopped or turned aside. All my life was that, when I lived. To be stopped, to be prevented.

I run at her. I leap. I seem to meet a rush of scalding fire and dense black mud, as if I'm in the trenches where so many men have died, but after, it is as if I pass through a blood-red sunset into a dawn of darkest shade.

How heavy I am. I weigh leaden on myself as an animal burdened beyond its capacity.

I sink down. The ground is kind to me. It holds me up. And over my eyes a drift of lemon – that is the colour – lemon – yellow silk, that is my hair, her hair, our hair – mine.

As once I did in life, I have fainted. But as I lie there unconscious, I sense I enter into her brain. Her own memories are gone, all but the fundamental mechanical lessons of how to see and speak and breathe and move and live. Her – my – heart is beating, slow but steady. Here is the place of many mansions.

I'd never realised, when alive before, to what a palace and playground we're given access in our own bodies. Now, I am again, I, and no other, *I* am the mistress of a splendid bodily house.

(*Coral*): We could not find the others. Elizabeth was kind, but eventually she went away. Everyone is outside, I think.

I have found a cupboard. I could not open the door, but I could pass through the door. Now I sit on the floor of the cupboard. I am crying. My tears are dry. Please, dear God, help me. There is no one else.

(*The Warrior*): The valiant old man has sent me on to my own quest.

Day is swole beyond the trees and golden, but I find none of the monster-creatures, so can mark none down. Are all their kind gone, as at the beginning they come and pass on? I may need to wait, but few have patience to want attendance upon afray when it stands due. God in his Mercie and pity, send me one I may try and have. Let this be done.

(*The Scholar*): I had anticipated the awful sense of stasis and heaviness, and duly braced myself for it and, once into the body, found soon I could bear it, knowing too I should grow accustomed, as are all living things, to the weight and unghostlike limits of their own bones and meat and blood.

The arm, luckily, set back as it should be, if in a flash of agony beyond my scope, (even the mortal smashing of my nose and skull seemed less than this healing pang, for they of course stunned me, lessening my awareness). But after a minute or two I apprehended what had happened. As I say, a wonderful piece of luck, due entirely to my forgetting, in that instant of achievement, that my new body's arm wasn't as it should be. Now in time it will repair, for there is certainly plenty of feeling in it – it aches and stabs from shoulder to palm. A trial. No matter.

It means the nerves have survived. I have bound it up by now, able to rend a piece from the body's – my – mess of shirt, now part of my inheritance! The feel of the horrible cloth, and of this bearded, unkempt wild thing's face and general skin, are a sort of Paradise to me. While this new vehicle of mine is around half a century, or close on, younger and more hale than my old model!

But then. The memory came. The soldier. And I wept.

I shall never forgive myself, though reason tells me it was not my fault. I didn't know the bomb would come.

But oh, to have *forgotten* – *that* is a worse crime, I believe. I will shoulder it, as I do the physical pain, as best I may.

To other events.

The Knight has left me, and I make out none of the others. I am sorry to say this fills me with relief. Now fixed as I am, *human*, as I am, I could see only steam and smoke where the Knight stood. Doubtless they will all be like this to me, now. If even I can see them at all, for we note, I'd never seen a ghost, not even here, before I died.

My best course perhaps is simply to stay put and wait. The rising sun seems to bring an unusual warmth – obviously, I haven't felt the heat of the sun for nearly a decade. The cold will be a nuisance. I mean to try to locate some clothing in the house. I have glimpsed wearable things here and there, hung in closets, but whether they will fit this stalwart fellow I am now become – fuck knows.

But then, Fuck knows everything, apparently. Fuck must be another of the three hundred and seventy names of God.

(*Elizabeth*): It's done. Nothing to it. Glide in, sink in my claws, subside in astonishment, sick in fact only with joy, and with revulsion only at the disgusting stink of it – of me, the Brand New Elizabeth. My God, what have I done! I double over with laughter. It hurts to laugh, as they told us, once. But it's a wonderful hurt. My choice, demonstrably, is outrageous. What will they all say? Who cares? They will get used to me, as I will. What a crazy thing – I have just pissed – And how *novel*! But aside from that, I'd forgotten the relief and sense of *achievement* merely passing water can provide. I look forward to the 'weightier' work, which old people, in my childhood, would refer to as Number Two.

I want to run for about a mile. But I'd better get the walking right before I try. I too, like this body before we met, have fallen over more than once in my insane and infantile rejoicings. But I'm strong as a bull and savage with – with what? With life, what else.

With LIFE.

(And one extra, wonderful thing. All the fingers of *this* body are intact, and function – unlike the damaged fingers I was left with that ruined my work last time. Plus the whole rig is strong as a camel.)

And then I think of my father.

I picture him, when I was fifteen, that handsome, elegant man, like an actor, but by then... more frail, a frailty I couldn't (wouldn't?) see, as to me he was eternal.

What would *he* say about what I've done, have *chosen* to do? He would hate it. He would be offended and startled, and perhaps attempt to hide that from me, sweet as he was, and liberal as he tried always to be.

I can recollect now, that thing that happened, those months before he died.

My pretty mother, you see, some four years younger than he and still in her thirties, had embarked on a little 'fling'. That is, she had gone off on holiday in America with some 'fascinating guy' she had met somewhere or other in London. It wasn't, she had said, 'an Affair'. Just something she 'needed to get out of her system', and so she 'sensibly' told us, my father first. I was shocked stupid and went to bits, and so he, my dad, stayed calm, and calmed *me* as much as he could. "These things happen," he said. "She's right. Get it done, and then we can go on as before." Which was what, I think, my lovely, clever, kind, filthy little bitch of a mother intended. (Like breaking a strict diet at Christmas, and virtuously resuming it afterwards.)

(When I asked my father if *he* had ever indulged in a 'fling', he looked in my eyes and quietly said, "No, Lizzie. I never needed to. I had everything I wanted here.")

She was gone a while. And while she was gone my appalled rage at her – which later I tried, and partly or totally succeeded in wiping off the slate of my mind – turned to a determinedly jealous wish she should never come back into our lives. Not mine. Not Dad's.

And I set up a sort of, well I can only call it a campaign. I have to make this clear: I wasn't incestuously sexually in love with my father. But I was *emotionally* in love with him. Always had been, always would be. In some ways still am. I'd tried, with some justification, to be what he would have me be, which was nothing bad at all – artistically bright, a little dramatic, glamorous, open to adventure and to thought. But with her having shown her true colours, evil, dirty ones at that, I began to try to shut her out. I suggested to him, 'tactfully' at first, then more boldly, that he too ought to have an affair or two. There must be lots of girls who'd be more than happy, etc. And I'm sure some would have been. My aim, however, was that he should have fun, and also take his revenge on my mother, closing her out, and turning instead to me – not for sex, obviously – but for intellectual and creative companionship. Elsewhere, outside, he would have sex. And *I* would be his platonic wife. What else did he require?

Only of course, you see, I was wrong. As a substitute

for my mother's company I was neither fitted nor – wanted.

In the end, one thundery miserable evening, in our new, miles-away, not-so-far-from-London house, he sat me down and told me flatly that No, he would not be having an 'affair' with anybody, did not want one, and fervently hoped I would stop mooting it, however much sophisticated kindness I intended. Also, I must stop cursing my mother, and trying, metaphorically, to paint her in such murky nasty tones. They did not, he said, suit either her, as portrait, or me as the painter. He needed, in fact, he told me, to be alone. Even I, he said, much as he loved me, was becoming – which word did he use? It wasn't any version of 'needy', nor 'exhausting' – I have fully eradicated the title or phrase for what he told me I was *not*, but *was* becoming.

In wretched silence I slunk away, and he took a train for the city. I barely saw him again until my mother returned, she a little crushed, which by then I couldn't even glory in. Awkwardly, we settled back, (ostensibly), to our former ways.

How odd it seems to me now, that I never ever questioned why my father, young enough, vital, active, was never called up to soldier in the Second World War. I have an idea I'd assumed what he did as a businessman was of so much use to the war effort, that he'd been told to keep on with it and leave the fighting to others. Nothing was ever said, and I know if he'd been sent I'd have been frightened crazy. Years and years after, in my thirties then, I'd had a horrible possible insight, which I'd brushed off me like a stinging insect; but it left a tiny dab of poison. Probably, honourable man that he was, he had tried to enlist. And then they must have found something just not quite right with his heart. And that was why, of course, of course, he'd never been thrown into the stye of battle. That was why I didn't lose him, my darling, *then*.

I remember I bustled off and bought the facsimile of the *Queen of the Night* aria, and wrapped it with care, hoping that once his birthday celebration arrived, things could reverse, at least for me, to normal. But of course he died, didn't he. He died the way most people do, it seems, leaving nothing behind for me, not even – his ghost.

I wish I hadn't thought of this again, sharp as if for the first, in such hollow depth, only an hour or so into my reborn life.

But perhaps it is an inevitable effect. The Zombie-brain is memory-emptied. And any new tenant of a home will want to fill up the bare cupboards. Will even begin to do it without quite being ready.

It's fresh for me again, now, my ridiculous and spiteful and pathetic lapse, his utter though gentle and controlled rejection of me. I wasn't enough. I wasn't her. It's shame, too, I feel. All my adult emotional existence after, I spent trying to replace my dad with worthless men, the beautiful, the pretty, the seemingly artistic and kind, and so many of them petty, ugly, and worthless–

That's why I unpacked this one memory. Or, this memory was finally able to hunt me down. Elizabeth, the black-haired fox, at bay now among the bones of another body, Elizabeth no longer.

It's that memory, even unremembered, it's that subsequent misjudgement of mine with all my male lovers, that's brought me to what I did tonight. That's why I chose as I did.

You, my father. Me, your daughter.

But now – no longer either.

(*Laurel*): We – I washed at the rill, and the cold was frightful. Yet too, I luxuriated in it – I can touch water, wash and drink, (all my new teeth are sound), I can feel the cold, shiver – and rub myself dry with grasses as I have only read of persons doing (briskly) in novels, long ago.

Already we are walking well, she and I.

I'll stop saying We and Our. I and my. *Me.*

At the house I will search out clothing. The historic show-clothes which remain will fall to bits if I attempt to sort, let alone put them on. It will have to be modern garments I take, with their uncorseted waists and short skirts. And trousers – How shall I feel then? Oh, like Heaven.

Only as I let myself in at one of the looser house doors, unable now to pass straight through, although for one silly moment I almost tried to! Only then memory came to me, a remembrance I didn't ever before recall, and don't properly, now... like something told to me, which, nevertheless, I must believe.

Captain Ashton, my beautiful captain, so brave and able, so couth and fine, who danced with me, as so seldom anyone did. Who left me, as did they all. Who, in my feverish dreams, as the virus known subsequently as Spanish 'Flu closed fast its talons on me, as on so many others – he, he too, died that night. He died since he had never lived. He was part of my fever-dream, that first night of my death. So real he seemed. So absolute that I have never doubted. But oh, like the fool I was – as never would such a man have paid court to me, become my lover, wed me, stayed with me – I dreamed him from the ashes of my evening, and of my life. My brain concocted him from nothingness. He wasn't real, my gallant captain, with his blue eyes and his moonlight hair. I changed my last living night for myself. I made it somewhat magical after all. Where, in fact, I'd sat as ever on that – what is it Elizabeth says? – that fucking chair. Sat as always I did, and died myself, early, of humiliation and loneliness. Oh, possibly a couple of diehards, egged on by embarrassed relations, took me for some loathsome, graceless flounder about the dance-floor. Maybe even one of them said he knew an aunt of mine, as if to prove I was safe with him – or more likely that never would he have danced with me at all if not requested. But he, my love, he never did. He wasn't real.

Oh, Laurel, what a glittering jewel your brain was then, no zircon, but a diamond of gleaming facets and silvery light, to conjure such a demon-angel lover to dance with you the dance of death, before the mansion of your life fell in.

But even I, we note, didn't lie to herself beyond a certain point. For in the fantasy he left me, too. He was polite, and just a touch equivocal. No more. Yes, even I, Laurel, the child of cold stone hearts, colder far than the spring-winter water morning, with its saffron sky and frost thick as thin snow, even I did not defraud myself to that extreme. My phantom love bestowed no kiss. He didn't clasp me to him, promised nothing. He bade me courteous and dry farewell.

More of a ghost than I, ever, Captain Ashton.

But now I am alive. My name isn't Laurel. I'll become again my true physical self. Daphne, before metamorphosis. Not quivering and cowering leaves, but a woman.

(*Coral*): -

(*The Warrior*): Sun is full risen and I see her, my Lady Eliseth – but she is other now. Though I know her still. Under the trees standing, and in a form that wounds me through. But it is her.

She – or the other now she is – that laughs at me.

Go on then, bold knight, she says. Down in the wood they are, the ones you seek.

A pass of birds, small as bees they seem to me, feathered arrow flights, passing over, and she or that-she-is looks up and laughs too at them, and so I behold she is not mocking either bird or this man before her. She laughs in gladness. She is happy then to be so at change, and other. Would it so then for me, I wish. With all my heart.

I pass, and go down the slope, stepping as I do as if I must. But my feet are not upon the world, but in air. And how I long for anchorage, to tread on ground. I will take any I may, it will not cost me, if it be to be again as alive, and touch whole earth under my feet.

It lies below a tall wilden holly, and the spikes of thissen and else have rent it.

Stand I and stare on it. The Sub-umbris is a corpse in all truth now? For never do we see, nor hear report, these things can diey. They are already of the dead.

As is the Scholar's choice, and my lady's, there is not

much seems amiss with this stricken enemie. Others of its kind trample a way off, avoiding maybe this one. Its eyes are open, blue, and now I see them turn on me. Makes sound, the lips of it. Has lost a tooth to one side. No impediment, I in life lost two, one deep in, that blackened and I pulled it forth, and one in fighting, but in the lower jaw.

I go near. I am stood above.

It makes a sound at me. But its both eye close now.

It is near death, and I not liking it, then surely the easier to leave it should I mean so.

It is of the male division, what else. Its hair is black as that of my Lord, when I served him, Hroldar, that Eliseth has call Rauldr, or some such. But the eyes as mine, in life. I stand, and by my will I reach inside.

Here it is this way: an empty tower. Its stones are firm and all in place, but through the vault of it the cele winds run like water in a stream.

I make testing of the spaces. None is there. One glimpsing sceadowe before me flies. It is a remembering, I think, of death. But that is done, as long far off was mine. Yet still I pause, thresholden, not yet to enter in.

And while my thought speaks to me, my life takes hold, and in like a spear of ice and fire, before ever I am ready, and so inside the towr of it am I.

Who now then will I be? I lie in fear, then to my feet I ream, lifting the lunk of me like a great wiht upon my soul. And stand I now, and solid as a tower may be, and my feet upon the back of the world, as Great God intended, flesh and blood and bone.

And then again I fall. The weight of him, of life – and there are memories – they run like rats, white and black and grey – and red. And with them, my own, my own, rising out of deep water.

I have the language now of this future place. I have the truth of my past. I am ruined, like the towers of the castle. Defeat and fall, if not death.

He – I – *hurt. I* hurt. There is rot all through him. Gangrene is its name. Inside a day or so, I'll die of the rot in him. Why did I never see in time? In my first life then, we had this evil rot, but now I can't remember its proper name – its name-of-then.

I lie, groaning, helpless. This ruined tower will die, and then I shall be free again. Or can I be? No second chances.

The pain is horrible.

I remember a pain as bad, and worse. Though did not last for long.

It was then, the battle, on the ramparts of the castle, my Lord's just fight –

Only –

I remember –

I remember.

The Fall of Leaf had come, and the weather yet very warm, the skies deep blue.

We were to fight the foes of my Lord. They sat below our fortress like mad dogs about a tree in which they had brought to bay something as powerful, but more so, than they.

But being crazed of course, they would come up to kill us. And so, a back door, as it might be, being undone for them, they duly do.

And then I am before my Lord. I cast off the foe from him and so his life is safe, but I in turn receive the blow, which is mortal and does for me. There we go. Done for. Always look on the bright side – these frills come from my host's dead brain-case. I speak like him. Or near to it for Christ's sake and damn this filth of pain in him – but I try to break away, and now I can't. Stuck in the mud of him, this Zombie. (Even without a tenant soul, still these dead bodies are able to die. They fall apart, as does the castle over yonder as, bit by bit, the house does too that was built here, with its green silks and old statues that aren't real...)

There instead am I, before my Lord. I take the blow for him and perish. And he lives.

But, to be honest. It wasn't like that.

Christ.

It wasn't like that.

Two months or more before that autumn, I had the spring fever common to these parts. The illness passed. But then came another skirmish, some unimportant little spat between my Lord and some other lord, some bugger with less right to hold an army than a fly. So on that day too I went to fight, I and fifty others. No more did we need. But on that day, that little new summer day, that day of stink and shit and hell, on that day some passing mace or other club came down upon me, and knocked me for six upon the ruck of grass, where I lay, not in my senses for some while, till gathered up.

And when again I came to myself, to myself I did not come, not I.

Do I remember this? In a manner. I heard a bell ringing in my head, over and over, on and on, till I would take a knife and stick it in my ear to stop the noise, yet some fool stops me. (There is always some fool will do that, sure. God makes fools for the very purpose.)

Let me be frank. To be honest. Lay my cards on the table.

From that dry tomorrow I was an idiot, a piece of flesh not a man, silly as a child of two. Weak as one. A fool forever.

Any other master would have slung me forth to whine and beg about the land, or for the holy women to care for, or the landsmen to jeer to death for a jolly wee laugh.

But my Lord, my Lord Raulder, he kept me on. Oh, no more his man, no more the guard of his body, the companion to toast at the feast: "My Gui – to you." As a hanger-on he kept me, to trail about the barracks, where men I had fought by, drunk by, swung through the brothels with and kneeled alongside at the holy Mass, might scorn me or be kind, or chafe at the omen of my fall: and wish me dead.

And so, in the fight upon the castle walk, where was I then?

Never beside my Lord, to serve and save, gladly to die for him if God willed it so.

No. In the yard below was I, gathering up the shed weapons and fallen stuff that might yet be of use to him, and those others yet men who could fight and save.

And there, like a ruined bird of prey, I picked around, gathering as I could, and only half aware, while overhead upon the stonework the insurge roared, flame flashed and blood flew free.

Gathering, pecking up, poor broken worthless bird, until an arrow, strayed from some otherwhere, out where the world was, and life and reason, shot through and into my world of sodden lolp and lack, and through my throat, so I choked and stifled, retching and cawing, and dropped dead. Useless to myself, and all.

And he above, my own God, Raulder, Hroldar, *he* fell. I *saw* him fall, and could not even cry or breathe or mourn, my windpipe all pierced through, and he pierced through his golden heart and through his silver soul. The wound I would, and happy, have borne for him. The wound of pride I was denied. Instead a wound of shame was mine, and is.

And when again I came to myself, and this time *was* myself, if a ghost, and less then than all and anything I had ever been, yes even as an idiot, *then* for myself I had changed the plot of the fucking story, hadn't I, bloody little lie-to-self cunt. Useless blundered fool. Like the cowards boasting in the tavern-pub of those brave, brave deeds and noble that they did and done and never done nor did, for real. None real. Me then, paur him. Poor bird.

Oh then formerly and forever let me die here and be done with all this crap.

(*The Scholar*): "My God!"I exclaimed. "Why – why on earth?"

Elizabeth was physically walking up the stairs, (as I, not so long ago, had already done). I knew her – but only in some aesthetic, intuitive fashion, maybe even psychic. There was no other possible way I could have done.

Like myself, she had become flesh and blood. She had pre-empted and assumed the body of a Zombie, and wore it now with swaggering *joi de vivre*. But – "My God," I said again. "What possessed you?"

"No, Matey," said Elizabeth. "I possessed this. Fine figure, don't you think? And look! Ten straight workable fingers. Impressed?"

"Uneasy," I said.

"Oh, come on, sir," said Elizabeth. "I've got the thing a bit together. But when it's fully scrubbed up and suitably garbed, we'll cut quite a figure."

"Elizabeth," I said, "you are a female. And that–"

"Is the body of a strapping young man. About early thirties, I'd say. Great hair, too, like black treacle. Just need to get it properly washed, and let it grow. About two feet, I think, yes? Down to the bum."

"You're a woman in the body of a man."

"And you, monsieur, are behind the times. I'm a ghost-soul in the body of a splendid living thing."

She was by then on the landing.

We stared at each other. I through the brown eyes that now were mine, and she through the (black treacle?) eyes of he she had assumed. He was, had been, perhaps could be again given her loving care, handsome. And strong, you could see, as an ox; perfect sculptor material.

"Why?" I said. Too late.

And gentle as the dove in the song, she said, "I was getting really sick of batting for the other team."

(*El*): How sweet he is, that old man. So astounded, yet still an open mind. The big old hunk he's now in looks good as a US tank for some forty years or more. Well done. And he operates it just fine. I'm doing well, too. Coordination, coordination.

He's told me his name, now, the one he's decided to answer to, which he admits isn't his own, but "that bit has passed".

He's Edward. Edward, our Scholar.

As for me, I'd better be El, (which sometimes I've been awarded as a nickname in the past, too, and then concluded was an abbreviation of Hell.)

So here I am, El or Hell, shaking Edward's hand! We can touch. Although, alas, I doubt I'll ever touch my Warrior-Knight now in any at-all intense way. I'll have to see how I feel about the Fair Sex, I suppose. (Fair Sex? Where the heck did *that* phrase come from? Oh, who cares?)

One thing that must be done. *Soon.*

I can see ghosts. I saw Laurel when she was – and I was *not* – and I hope, and think she's something else by now, but have to wait to confirm this. Not sure Edward the Scholar *can* see ghosts now he's flesh again. My Knight – I'm not sure either. And if he could, can he still, if he made it into that excellent Zombie I spotted and directed him to? No news yet there, either.

(Why am I so confident? The drunken exhilaration of achieving what one *must*. Like the splendid result of a supremely-needed exam.)

But to return to earlier things. I, or I and the Knight whoever now he is – must try to find little Coral. I'm worried about her. And she's still – well, as we all were not long ago – a ghost. We have to try to reassure and coax her. She's part of the family. You don't desert them.

No, Mummy, you don't.

And darling, sweet Father, forgive me, I knew not what I did. If ever again I find you, we'll sort it out.

I love you.

I'll always love you.

But my time of loss and remorse, guilt and blindness, some twenty-five years of it – and more, more – together nearly eighty – is it? – years. And that's over. I'm a different person now. Aren't I, my black-haired darling, aren't I, boyo? Giddy-up, my fine stallion! On to the

Dance Floor of Life!

(*Daphne*): I go up the main staircase. My feet still feel like weights of lead, but that too is wonderful in its way! And I can breathe! I touch the banister, and run my hand along it. Neglected and in bad repair, a splinter cuts into my palm. I rake it out, and there's a little speck of red, red blood. I am proud of the blood. All is as it should be.

I believe I shall manage the lack of two fingers on my left hand quite well, since for so long I've had no true tactile contact with anything, and am re-learning how to touch and balance and position myself in relation to all other things, which seems to be rather as a child first learns to do it, and so the disadvantage with the hand will simply be taken into account automatically.

I wonder if Coral is less afraid? I'm concerned about her. Or has she gained courage and found a suitable host for herself?

I notice I am much taller like this than I was as Laurel. Daphne, even barefoot, is a good five feet eight inches in height.

I must find some proper clothing. It's far too cold to go about like this. And there are old shampoos in one of the modern bathrooms. I shall take one to the rill and wash my hair properly.

On my right thigh there's a sore place. When I first noted it, I was disturbed, thinking it might be some sort of decay of the Zomboid flesh. But I saw not long ago that it's healing. The healing is very fast.

But I must find Elizabeth. Has she been able to change yet? I thought she couldn't bring herself to it – but she's so brave and wonderfully wilful, I think now she has. I'll find her, and together then we will seek and find Coral. Will I though be *able* to see any of them still? Now I'm flesh again, and if they so far are not? If Elizabeth – is not...

(*Coral*): My father.

I curl up here inside the cupboard, and I hear them stamping about the house. Bees. They have all become the Z-thing bees from the wilds outside. Even Elizabeth has done it. Even she.

I am all alone, and forever.

My father...

My mind is coiling and turning about and around itself like a snake.

I can only think at last of that night, the night I was killed, there in my cold little bed. All this while, years, decades, I have known Miss Archer murdered me. But, of course, it was never Miss Archer. She was a lovely little clever brainless fool, my father's dupe and concubine. But it was he who stole into my room and clamped the pillow tight and immoveable to my near-sleeping face. It was his strength, the strength of a determined and pitiless man, that crushed out my life. And that stench of dark and heated metal was, too, the reek of that same villainous vile man at his work. My dearest mother had left in trust for me some little inheritance or other, but he would gain it all if I should die. And so he took care my signature was always current on the documents. And when the hour was at its best he snuffed me out like the fragile candle I was. No doubt, she, Miss Archer, was his accomplice, at least in telling everyone how sickly I had always been, had caught a chill despite her constant wise admonitions to take care, had evidently succumbed to it, and my own pathetic frailty, in the night, when she and he had been innocently at the piano, playing and singing virtuous songs of honourable, self-sacrificing love and pious valour. In fact they would have been at other games; his murderous paws, that had just dispensed with me, washed themselves clean in the romantic dews of her passion, as he – what does Elizabeth say? – fokked her senseless. Did she know or guess he had murdered me? She was, under her teacher-cleverness, a dolt, a 'twit' as Elizabeth might say. Or if she did deduce his perfidy, probably she was too greedy to reveal it.

He should have swung on the fokking gallows, my rat of a father. At least now he rots in some hole in the ground. While I have lived, admittedly in a limited and insubstantial, wispy way. But I have lived. Nor do I suffer in Hell for the unspeakable crime of filiacide, as is the other possibility for him, should Hell at all exist.

Why I came to this revelation here, in my cupboard, I do not know. But I feel perhaps it is good that I have. It has freed me of some shackling chain I never realised lay on me. It has released me to become, perhaps, myself, whomsoever that may be.

I will not call her 'Coral' any more. That is for sure. Coral is pink and brittle and may break. No, I shall be Cora, which I know in Greek, or believe I know it, means *Maiden*. Which I am. A maiden. Then, I am Cora.

Then, Cora, shall we after all rise up and pass through the cupboard door, and see what they have become, our loving friends, now Z-bees? For after all, somehow I have survived, in spirit, the stinking claws of a murderer, and in spirit still I can survive all else. Rise up, then, Cora. Let us proceed.

Outside, I see him instantly. He climbs the stair and comes along the passage slowly, as if the effort makes him ache. And – how curious – though not at all now as he was, I know this is our Knight, and too, now, I know his name is Gui, a name of old France.

Seeing me, for see me he does, a slow smile rises through his much-different face. His eyes are blue, however, as before, and he looks out from their windows, and gradually, moment by moment, he is becoming more and more himself.

"What a brave girl you are," he says to me, and I understand his words, as I never before did. "I'm so glad to see you, and the others will be glad. But I have some news, though I'll wait a while to tell you. Let's find Eliseth, and the rest of them, first. Come dear, come with me."

His voice is like that of a true father. If I could, I would put my hand in his.

(*Gui*): That ground was hard, in the aftermath of the battle. The battle with my own lie, and with the real facts. And I was rotten, though not with self-blindness, but gangrene. Sheer mortal decay. When the stinging and tingling began, I believed it was the end of me. I would not cry out, but writhe there, and shadows closed over me, as, in that other death, there had been no time for me to feel.

When peace poured through, water through a dirty drain, I opened up my eyes, and saw, over by a tree bending with its own foliage, a young woman sat. Clearly she was mindless, one of the foe, even so not raging or lumbering and intent on harm. Perhaps she took me for one of her own clan, the monsters, for I had drawn on the body of one such.

Then up is she, and runs fleet as a deer. But I am better it seems. And so I get to my feet, and pain it assails me, but for Christ's sake not as it was. I judge then from the few wounds taken of enemies in my former human life, that I have healed, heal still, but mended I am, or will soon be.

Why this is, God He may know.

I think, frankly, it's just the influx of ghost-life, revving up the dormant brain and immune system, kicking health back into touch, where for the unoccupied Zombie, empty of life-force, operating on overdrive, such abilities are gone.

As I go slowly then back towards the house, I pass again the girl like a running deer. She is small and slender, with a lost sad face. Nothing in her bright eyes, except – what is it there? And of which of them does she remind me? I know. This maid is like Coral. Well, then, perhaps...

When I am in, and find her in the corridor, I see her plain, as before. It seems I shall be like Eliseth, or what Eliseth has become – a man? On God's earth – but still she can see ghosts, as I now do.

I wish I might take Coral's hand to lead her down, but cannot, she being yet as she is. But she smiles at me her cautious little smile.

"Does it hurt to go into them?" she asks of me.

"No," I say. "It's strange – and sometimes there are past injuries–" I try for words to encourage and not affright her, "But they heal, and well and swiftly. You need only be brave a moment." How I hope for her this will be so.

But she says, "I am a coward. Afraid of everything, always."

"The coward," I answer, "is the bravest of any, if he will act despite his fear. While the hero has no work that way at all."

At a window, we pause. "Look, do you see?"

For there below, on the lawn of unkempt grass, the deerlike girl stands, as if – waiting. As if that body, soulless and mindless, yet sees that life is due to come back. If it is.

Coral looks out. "She is like me," says Coral. And then, "When I am her I shall be Cora. Will you be kind to me still?"

"Ever and always, dear Cora."

And she drifts out through the window, dropping soft as thistledown, as mist and light, over and into and away within the waiting vessel there beneath. So Eve, entering the clay about the rib of Man. So the soul entering the chosen child. So the spirit through the Needle's Eye.

PART FIVE

Edward, El, Daphne, Cora and Guy

They have found biscuits, which are hard and stale, and canned fish that seems all right, and tea and coffee which are still viable, once the water has been heated over the big fire they have laid, and lit with matches. For a wonder, the chimney doesn't catch alight, perhaps mostly because they wouldn't care if it did. There are bottles of red wine, which has lasted, and even a magnum of Champagne, which bubbles out green, and buzzes in the mouth, but seems not bad, if not as good, probably, as when it was laid down in 2010. The cellars are in an awful state but they've rummaged through, laughing and cursing. When loose bits of ceiling and endless cobwebs fell on them, or outraged mice tore over their feet, they shouted with joy – they can *feel*, they can smell and taste, their skins are scratchable by debris, and their eyes water at the dust.

The party goes on through the day into the dark, and across midnight. Their acquired bodies stand up to the onslaught quite well. Only Daphne is sick – the Champagne – and recovers quickly via the dose of brandy El furnishes from an old black bottle. (El also held Daphne's head while she threw up. El didn't seem to mind. After, El stroked Daphne's yellow hair and said he (he now, El) was going to call Daphne *not* Daphne, but Daffodil, for this succulent hair.) "I'll paint you, Baby," said El. "You're a beauty. A grand example of the fair sex." And El thought, *You filthy wretch, you body. Down boy. Don't freak her out.* But Daphne the Daffodil blushes through her body's weather-caught tan, and doesn't seem

unduly to mind. Gui and Edward play cards, and teach
Cora to play Patience, and Poker, and Gui says he thinks
his body must have played cards before, for how else
does Gui know these games?

They sleep in batches from about 3 a.m. onward. Gui
and Cora go to look at the sinking stars near dawn.
Edward lies on his back on the long table, with a cushion
under his head, snoring a little, and hearing himself
snore, and loving the noise of a proper throat.

Next day, with childish glee, they all (though
decorously in private) perform their natural functions,
marvelling nearly religiously over the results, (even
Daphne had been unsuitably fascinated a moment by her
sick). They wash in barely heated water, lave on
deodorants and hair-gels, and nearly choke themselves
with slurps of toothpaste and harsh new brushes. From
ransacked closets, they dress in a comic parade selection
of clothes ranging, roughly, between the slightly
threadbare 1950's and the outrageously over-retro styles
of 2019.

Oh the pleasures of the physical. How had they ever
grown bored with these toys? Never, never again. Not so
long as they live, which they each intend to do now – if
not forever – then for as near as makes no difference.

But it's possible, isn't it, one way or another, these
newly acquired living vehicles the heroes have annexed
may die – of natural causes – war, accident, disease,
murder, age... Even perhaps, for whatever now-
unpredicted reason, one or other of them may one day
kill the body he or she now has on, which at this present
time they value so highly. Who can foresee? And what
then? To be a ghost again, and maybe seek another re-
housing project? Or flying elsewhere to other ills or

blessings of which they can know nothing, here. But let that go for now. Now is the Present, the Gift of Today, and there can be Champagne, if not quite up to standard, and every hand can hold a glass, or a toothbrush, or a doll, or a sword or a rose. Or another hand. And the fire burns bright.

Later, over toasted loft-stored apples and mugs of tea, they discuss the journeys they will make next. Perhaps there are other centres of live un-Zombied people, or even people reclaimed from Zombishness by an influx of ghosts similar to their own invasion force.

They have a sing-song round an out-of-tune piano, (played by El), in which Cora's dolls join. Gui manages to call El 'El'. He'll get better at that. He's decided to spell his own name in the English way: Guy.

It rains, and they – and the dolls – go out to roll about in their nice new clothes. Children again.

(They know instinctively they have been miraculously lucky in discovering – or having presented before them – such almost perfect new domiciles, (bodies). The luck they never question. It's theirs by right. And so perhaps it is... unless some magnetic need of theirs has drawn ideal specimens towards them here. Rather as El and Ed used to make the lights work –)

At some other juncture they know, one and all, they must leave the house, and begin the follow-up adventure of their rebirth. A family, and such a close one, they are of one mind.

El kisses Daphne Daffodil under a tree, going slowly because DD grew up in the early 1900s, not the 1960s. And DD blushes, and holds El's hand. Guy begins to teach Cora old French, and she begins ably to learn it. He lost a daughter once, still-born. But here is another daughter, and she'll grow up – her body is about sixteen, seventeen. As he, he supposes, will grow old. He will be glad to do so. He's had no bloody chance to grow old before. And killing enemies? Well, one he has successfully repossessed. He's more eager now to assist his friends.

As for old Edward, (now about fifty-seven), he has found a family, but also a pipe and some tobacco – bollocks to the deteriorated and poisonous cigarettes electrically shorted out, or growing verdigris in the stores. He had smoked a pipe at Murchester, and elsewhere, until the hoo-ha about smoking turned everyone into a frustrated monk. Who cares now? Who cares?

Life is for the living. Live and let live.

And so they do. Soon out into the wide world they will go, bold as brass and twice as bright. The sun's rising again, strawberry and honey. And this tomorrow is, and will be always, another day.

It matters not how strait the gate,
How charged with punishments the scroll,
I am the Master of my Fate:
I am the Captain of my Soul.

Invictus

W.E. Henley

(1849 - 1903)

EPILOGUE

The Recluse

Today I will thank God, nay, I shall heap upon the Lord ten thousand praises: They are gone. How I have lamented and suffered this while, these endless years, nigh on three hundred of them.

At the commencement, the intrusion seemed not too onerous a burden upon me, for only one in number was there to haunt my peace, and that one inclined also to keep mostly to himself in the purlieus of the old castle. Yet then, in ones and twos, the rest were added unto him, until at length full five of the beasts had taken up their residence within my private lair. I could step nowise and nowhere without I must chance upon some other. I, who throughout his existence, quick or dead, have loathed and shunned the company of what simpletons are apt to call My Fellow Man. Tush. I have no fellow, nor he me. The last of them also proved the worst, too, since he drove me out my library wherefrom, until that hour, none ever had, neither ghost nor man. For most living presences grew invisible to me, when once I had become a phantom, and inaudible too. As indeed I must conclude I grew for most of them. Nor had this fiend troubled me, while yet he lived. But following his doubtless deserved demise, we were in another case quite. A ghost by then, as am I, his continual adherence to my own preferred retreat, my hermitical cell, caused me to conceal myself yet more, especially from him, and then into exile I take myself, to the lower depths of this, once my, house. And there, ten or more long years, I have clung, pitiable as a bat upon the darkness' wall. In hiding, cursing my lot, nor no respite in view.

During this winter of my discontent, creatures of vile aspect began to swarm across the land outside. They are not Men, as not quite living – since, as a ghost, as I have said, full-living men, nor women, I seem not to see. But these things, a sort of golem, I do. They have a name also, which I have partly heard, as if spoken on the wind, *Zumble* I believe it to be; but they are monsters that prowl.

Then commences a miracle. The ghostly five presences here inflicted upon me are able, it turns out, to enter and possess the Zumble Kind. Thus my torturers pass from the state of spirit back to flesh, if so it may be termed, and imbued with fleshly form and motion they are apt to desert my house and rove the country beyond. There is, for myself, this added curiousness: while the Zumble Kind are, for me, both visible and somewhat obscure – when once occupied by the five ghostly parasites who had infested here, the five chosen Zumble creatures dim out from my sight, as does a flame beneath the hood of a smoke-dirtied lamp. To their discredit, their noise is still audible to me, as that of men generally is not. But even the noise grows muted. Until there comes a congruence of days and darknesses, and then, to my joy, all five enghosted Zumbles depart.

For sure, I have no interest in any man, nor female either, save their history comes to me within the covers of a book. By concentration only I see my tormentors leave, one fine day's break, passing away down the hill, unsightly outlines, as of sacks of vaporous skin that walk and talk, yet fainter with each beat of my silent heart, and so they vanish into the view, as water soaks in earth.

Thank God, I say, nought else but ten thousand praises be upon the Lord.

This then of myself I will say: my father inherited this house from my grandsire, on the death of the same. My mother dwelled selectly, by then, in London, and since I was nine years I saw but little of her, nor wished more. For my schooling, my father, Francis Hollander, engaged tutors to lesson me privately, and though I liked none of them, and two were perfect clodpolls, I learned sufficient for my purpose, and did not need to mingle with other persons. My father, here, had some understanding of my preference. Nay, I am sure he himself had no fondness for company, not mine, nor my mother's, nor that of any other one. Perhaps I shall expand briefly on this theme. I have one short memory of the woman, my dam, spurning a painting of the Virgin Mother and Jesus, her Son, She holding the Messiah in a loving coil of light, to protect and worship, both. My mother's contempt was not, it seems, for religion. Rather this woman disliked merely the concept of maternal love. To this hour, I carry marks which attest to that theory. Her personal harshness to me was of such vividity that even as a ghost, I keep the scars. For him, the man I must assume had sired me, best he liked to walk about the grounds here, to shoot a little, and now and then to fish from the quiet pools. Unlike myself, he was not much drawn to reading. Instead he would write out books himself, for perchance he felt no other scribe could match him in awarding to him pleasure. Some of his works, I believe, he published, under some one or two false *nom de plume*, as the French rabble have it. I remember that we did not breakfast, nor dine together, but I would meet him sometimes in the house;

our exchange at this, for my part carefully respectful, and voiceless on his, would last no longer than a minute, if so great a while. At occasion, he might have music. But he would then have the musicians taken to a certain room, and there let a servant serve them with food and alcohol, and after this they would play, out of his sight, but the music to be heard by him, elsewhere. This wise custom of his I too adopted, in my adult years, when he in turn had gone to earth in his grave. Like him, also, I had a favourite coat, mine of a greenish brocade, which I would wear when in my library, though more sober clothes at supper; during which, as with my sire, only one servant waited upon me, and silent as the tempered night. So I lived nicely in my house, but in my own order must at length meet that fatallest Hour of Death. So I woke from a peaceful slumber in my forty-ninth year, and getting up from my bed, learned yet I lay in it. Some time I was bemused, but then far less, seeing no demand had come with my end that I rush elsewhere, into some Heaven or Hell awash with dead humanity at its loudest and least desired of me. Then too, I gave my thanks to God. Yes, even though I could no longer open my books to read them, for I was secure enough, and so required them less, having no otherwhere from which to flee to them in fear.

Later also, when a descendant of our line infected the house with himself, and thence a brood of some sixteen children, seeing I never noted them after my first dismay, nor they took heed of me, there also I gave thanks. The first years of my Bliss scarcely ever disturbed – save, and this not of frequency, by the ancient warrior ghost in mail, from whom I hid. My horror at the later invasion therefore, by those other phantom Children of Adam, may now be better apprehended. And thus, as so it has fallen all are gone – my ecstasy and true relief.

Now and forever, let me be alone. It is all I ask.

Villainous Fate! O pitiless Contrivance! Tell me only how a dead man may die, and I will work it for me! Must I, still sensible of All, crawl under the earth into a grave! So then it shall be.

In the last sunset of a month of leaf fall, when the castle ruin and the sinking house glowed yellow as tarnished ormolu, from a high window, I saw a shape upon the sward. Let me be plain in what I saw. Much of a year had passed since my liberation. I had counted it in days and even in hours, like a miser with his hoard of precious coins. During this while also, the soulless prowling of those other dead-living things about the grounds had eased. For, despite being somewhat unaware of them, their general absence did make itself felt by me. Such happiness this gave me, at all lack of company.

On that night, however, as the golden glister faded into twilight, I saw, as clearly as the drawn blade of a knife, what wended toward my sanctuary. And yet, too, not quite clear enough. For what might it be that the figure was? And, too, what strayed about with it as it came on, winding around it somewhat, and now pulling in close, or else unwound a little distance off, yet the larger figure always keeping it by, so it would seem held upon some kind of flimsy rope? Is it that the greater form is that of a woman? And is it too that she has a hound upon a leash? But she, and it also, the dog, are phantasmal, for though solid enough when stared upon by me, yet the last ray of the sun gleams through them both, and sceptic as I am, I see it too. Two ghost things come again to plague me, then. I am betrayed.

Mother And Child

Such a way we com.

And all alone. Just him and me.

Corse, no food or nothn. But he dont, and I dont, need to eat or nothn. Not now.

Fuckin weird tho. Still not used to it. He ent scared tho. Genius he is. He trusts me. Hes had to, like, what else. Sory for the words. I never got learned to read. Nor talk like, if it com to that. Dont want to say bout my life ifor I died.

For that zomby thing got hol of us. It was all shit wern it.

Tryn to git outa Londun we was and walkn on the ralway line cos no trains no mor was ther. And we was OK but then this zomby com out one of them shed things and I cant run, Im too big and heavy by then and it slams its fist in my face, like a thouznd fuckers hav, but I spos it breaks my nek and so we, me and my darlin, are ly on the trak and it eats a bit of me then wonder off of the line. Later I cum to and Im dead and Im nother of them – nother zomby, and so I spose he is, my lovly boy. So we go on agane, on up the trak. Walks miles we dun and then the citys gon and after we clime the slope up and go on along the rode.

Weeks, walkn. And then somethin but I dont kno whot. We just wore out maibe. Died agan, praps. Mustve. Both of uz.

But when we cum to next we rize up, him and me, and wer gostes.Weer goests. But wot we leeve behind on the rode is wot wed turn into, zomby thing, me and him. Ded as dedd. Onl stil alive this gost way, we twoo. Him and me. Nevr be parted now, I luv him so, and him me. Hes only one evr lov me. His farther nevr dun. Just one time in the back of a stole car. And by the time I kno whot happn, wurlds falln apart. But him here still with me always. He dont mind it. He say so, onli not in wurds. I call him Aragorn. Dont kno what name com from, just remembr it like. I like that name. I can spel it.

Look at him. Evn like thiz hes lovli. Bles. Bless him. Im so glad Im not aloen.

Lot of the tyme he get carrid inside me, corse. But nown then he com out and walks with me. But I hold the burthcaud – they tol me wot it waz at the hospatl – the Umbillycal Corde – just to gyde him like keep him close, in case. An he turn and laufs at me, and he makes the caud twang like a stringg on a gutar. An we both lauf then. Dont hurt, him or me. And inside, when I carry him that way hes not hevy or weari me. I lov him so. At night, tho we don slepe, he settles back in me and I hold him in my belli with my arms, and ysee we can touch. I dont knoe how cos weer gostes and we just pass thru stuff, tree and wals, but he and me can touch. Paps coz weer stil part of each over. Hes warm and he says I am, onli not in werds. Aragorn. My Sun.

Theres a bildin heer. Big ol plays and we stand at the dore as darknis cum. We culd pass strait in, but we dont.

Remind me of a stori my gran tol me wen I was little. She tolt me to scair me, shee was crule, like. But I nevr forget. Sum gurl go in a dor of a bigg hows, an thiz gyant com and ait her up.

So we don go in, nor nock.

We just wayte.

An starz cum on in the skie like diemonds.

The Recluse

In the Name of the Highest, it is not a dog on leash. It is –
it is a child of her womb unborne, and still enchained to
her by the cord of birth! But it moves outside her, and
she, to keep it safe, holds to the cord with one hand.
There is no wound nor schism. They are as one.

The child is an embryo of perhaps seven months
maturing, yet one may make out its features; also that it is
male. The cord itself is, too, uncommonly, monstrously
long, and very flexible, silvery in colour, like woven
smoke.

They do not enter my house. I, by the upper casement,
stare down on them. They are seated together on the
narrow terrace. They seem to watch the stars of Heaven.
It comes to me, in the silence of the gathering night, that
once I too was a child within the body of a woman. But
she, bringing me forth with pain and exertion, had
thereafter no liking for me, and punished me for it. And
for the matter of that, therefore, had I no liking for her, or
any.

The moon rises late, almost at her full, milk pale, and
they, these two, look up, and she murmurs to the child,
and he lifts up his hand, smaller than the paw of a kitten,
and he waves to the moon in greeting. And then – ah
God! – Turning about he waves to me.

Mother and Child

An old man in a grene cote has com down and out the door and show us we can go in. And Aragorn duz, so I must.

The old man has funny hair, like in telly series – curli and stiff, wiv powda in it. Dont kno.

Like TV movi inside the hous an all, like the ol stuff they show for the lectricks go. But Aragorn is like pleesed. The ol man duznt do nothin bad. Only he stand by the wal and hes cryn, but his teers arnt wet. But he crys on and on, and the teers like diemonts or stars. But Aragorn drag me, and when he get cloze, he lifts up a bit in the air and his hand up to the ol mans cheek.

Thers no touch. Cant be, onli he an me can touch won another. But the old man looks at him, and then he sits down, the ol man, on the posh old floor, and Aragorn sits rite by him, and so do I. Its not bad then, sort of peecefull. Sort of like some other thing I dont kno wot. And we watch the big moon together thru a windowe, not wet, but like a white whyt teer.

So the darkness shall be the light,
and the stillness the dancing.
Four Quartets
T.S. Eliot
(1888 - 1965)

About the Author

Tanith Lee was born in North London (UK) in 1947. Because her parents were professional dancers (ballroom, Latin American) and had to live where the work was, she attended a number of truly terrible schools, and didn't learn to read – she is also dyslectic – until almost age 8. And then only because her father taught her. This opened the world of books to Lee, and by 9 she was writing. After much better education at a grammar school, Lee went on to work in a library. This was followed by various other jobs – shop assistant, waitress, clerk – plus a year at art college when she was 25-26. In 1974 this mosaic ended when DAW Books of America, under the leadership of Donald A Wollheim, bought and published Lee's *The Birthgrave*, and thereafter 26 of her novels and collections.

Since then Lee has written around 95 books, and over 300 short stories. 4 of her radio plays have been broadcast by the BBC; she also wrote 2 episodes (*Sarcophagus* and *Sand*) for the TV series *Blake's 7*. Some of her stories regularly get read on Radio 4 Extra.

Lee writes in many styles in and across many genres, including Horror, SF and Fantasy, Historical, Detective, Contemporary-Psychological, Children and Young Adult. Her preoccupation, though, is always people.

In 1992 she married the writer-artist-photographer John Kaiine, her companion since 1987. They live on the Sussex Weald, near the sea, in a house full of books and plants, with two black and white overlords called cats.

Also From Immanion Press

Ghosteria

Volume One: The Stories

Tanith Lee

ISBN 978-1-907737-61-9
IP0118
£10.99, $19.99

In this new collection, which contains most of the ghost stories of Tanith Lee – including 4 new tales original to this volume – Lee slips freely through the full gamut of Fantasy, SF, Horror, Historical, Parallel and Contemporary genres. The themes range, amongst others, with a lost love in early 20th Century New Zealand, a bullied child in 1970's India, into the underhill palace of a brooding magician in search of wonders, among the guests of a modern spiky wedding-breakfast, and beside a psychic, on a far planet whose damson skies are adrift with flying whales...

The moods conjured are dark, unnerving or plain nasty; or else sad, tender, kind and - now and then – outright crazy.

Turn up the light
And don't look behind you.

NewCon Press

http://newconpress.co.uk/

The very best in fantasy, science fiction, and horror

Colder Greyer Stones by Tanith Lee

Released to commemorate the author being honoured with a Lifetime Achievement Award at the 2013 World Fantasy Convention, this stunning collection of stories provides further evidence of why Tanith Lee is held in such high regard by fans and contemporaries alike. The book features twelve wonderful, rich-textured tales including the brand new novelette "The Frost Watcher" and five stories previously available only in the (sold out) signed limited edition "Cold Grey Stones".

Paperback: ISBN 978-1-907069-60-4   £9.99

The Moon King by Neil Williamson

"Beautifully written and thoughtful… one of the best debuts of this or any other year." – *Jeff Vandermeer*

"The Moon King is literary fantasy at its best." – *The Guardian*

Life under the moon has always been predictable: day follows night, wax phases to wane and, after the despair of every Darkday, a person's mood soars to euphoria at Full. So it has been for the five hundred years since Glassholm was founded, but now all that has changed. Amidst rumours of unsettling dreams and strange whispering children, society is disintegrating into unrest and violence. Three people find themselves at the eye of the storm: a former policeman investigating a series of macabre murders, an artist embroiled in the intrigues of revolution, and a renegade engineer tasked with fixing the ancient machine at the city's heart…

Paperback: ISBN 978-1-907069-62-8   £12.99

Other Immanion Press Titles by Tanith Lee

The Colouring Book Series

Psychological tales and unsettling histories...

Greyglass 9781907737046 £10.99
The house... always growing, adding to itself, blooming, decaying, becoming reborn... But Susan doesn't live in the house of Catherine, her grandmother. When Catherine dies, no one mourns. The house is always changing. As if at last it must achieve some irresistible transformation. Frankly, there is something *uncanny* about the house. Isn't there.

To Indigo 9781907737213 £11.99
Don't talk to strangers. Don't even look at them. Novelist Roy Phipps leads an uneventful existence in the house inherited from his parents. His only aberration is the story he's been secretively writing for years of the mad poet Vilmos, a study of murder, angst and alchemic magic. Then one evening Roy meets Vilmos, face to face. As shadows close in on him, Roy understands he's now fighting for his own sanity. And probably his life.

L'Amber 9781907737251 £11.99
Jay has very little. Jilaine Best has everything. But even Jilane's perfect life is flawed, longing for the baby she's unable to conceive. She's willing to let another woman give birth for her. And so Jay confesses she is already pregnant with an unwanted child. Lies are so easy to tell, if you've had enough practice. Harder to change into truth. Spin your web. Watch it tangle. Now see what you've caught.

Killing Violets 9781907737367 £10.99
1934... Starving to death somewhere in Europe, Anna meets Raoul, who takes her to England and the dubious mansion of his arrogant and unsavoury relatives, the Basultes. Anna is a survivor. Both the aristocratic malignities, and the Hogarthian orgies of the servants,

can be accommodated, if they must. Anna has a past as savage and explicit as anything seen in the Basulte house.

Ivoria 9781907737404 £11.99
Nick Lewis certainly has no liking for his TV historian brother, Laurence. Aside from anything else Nick blames him for the death of their mother, the beautiful actress Claudia Martin. And so, is it possible the off-handedly childish trick played by Nick on Laurence really does cast some kind of curse? This is probably *not* a supernatural story. It might be less unsettling if it was.

Cruel Pink 9781907737497 £11.99
Emenie, a serial killer, lives alone. She can read omens and knows exactly her legitimate prey. Rod has a dreary life, working at an unrewarding job with something uneasy hanging over him. Is it the wardrobe? Klova is young, beautiful, living on benign handouts, in a Science Fantasy existence of sprints and liquid-silver...Until she meets the challenging Coal. Here, at the outskirts of this City they all call London, what the Hell is going on?

Turquoiselle 9781907737596 £11.99 *Also in Kindle Ebook*
Not much is what it seems. The job can be dull, but quite demanding. The work is lucrative, however. He can easily afford the costly wants of Donna, his partner. It's just that suddenly things are running less smoothly. This stuff with Donna... Various unusual tensions at work... the bizarre and threatening business over Silvia... In the end, maybe all you can rely on is yourself.

And In Ebook Through Kindle

Kill the Dead
Night's Master
Death's Master
Delusion's Master
Delirium's Mistress
Turquoiselle
Ghosteria Volume 1: The Stories

CPSIA information can be obtained
at www.ICGtesting.com
Printed in the USA
FSOW01n0659221015
12469FS

9 781907 737633